APR      2005

MW01017585

# DAMN YANKEES

## CASEY, WHITEY,

## YOGI, AND THE MICK

HIGHSMITH 45-220

GAYLORD S

Photographs ©: AP/Wide World Photos: 73, 83, 128; Corbis-Bettmann: 26, 96; Courtesy of National Baseball Hall of Fame and Museum, Inc.: 60; National Baseball Hall of Fame Library, Cooperstown, NY: 104; Transcendental Graphics: 12, 44, 65; UPI/Corbis-Bettmann: 7, 17, 35, 61, 68, 88, 113, 121, 122, 133, 135.

Library of Congress Cataloging-in-Publication Data

Gilbert, Thomas W.
     Damn Yankees : Casey, Whitey, Yogi, and the Mick / Thomas
Gilbert.
         p.   cm. — (The American game)
     Includes bibliographical references and index.
     Summary: A history of baseball from 1949–1964, focusing on the
incredible New York Yankees who won fourteen of sixteen American
League pennants and became champions of the world nine times.
     ISBN: 0-531-11338-8
     1. New York Yankees (Baseball team)—History—Juvenile literature. [1.
New York Yankees (Baseball team)—History. 2. Baseball—History.] I. Title. II.
Series: Gilbert, Thomas W. American game.
     GV875.N4G55   1997
     796.357'64'097471—dc21                                    97-3492
                                                                   CIP
                                                                   AC

# CONTENTS

# Tv, Pinstripes, and Backyard Barbecues: Post-War America and the Yankees Run up the Score

A lot of baseball fans thought the Yankees were at the end of the line in 1948. After a run of seven American League pennants in eight years under venerated manager Joe McCarthy, the team had won only one pennant in the past five seasons. The reason for the Yankees' decline seemed obvious: the men responsible for the glory days of the 1930s were gone. McCarthy was now managing the hated Boston Red Sox. Hall-of-Fame first baseman Lou Gehrig was dead. So was owner Jacob Ruppert, the man who had paid the extravagant salaries of Ruth and Gehrig. Team president Ed Barrow, the genius behind the Yankees front office and scouting organization, had been pushed aside by minority club owner Larry MacPhail. As if to underline the team's break from its own winning tradition, Babe Ruth passed away in August 1948 from throat cancer; decades of drinking, smoking, and burning the candle at both ends had caught up with him at 53.

The player who succeeded Ruth in the hearts of New York fans, Joe DiMaggio, played in splendid physical shape and took much better care of himself off the field than Ruth had. Unfortunately, DiMaggio found that his graceful body was beginning to betray him in 1948, at the young age of 33. Battling against excruciating pain caused by a bone spur in his right heel, DiMaggio had his last great season that year, batting .320 with 39 homers and 155 RBIs. DiMaggio's courage, however, made little difference in the pennant race. New York finished third, trailing both Cleveland and Boston, under easygoing "players' manager" Bucky Harris.

No one was surprised when the shake-up came. Bought out by Del Webb, a contractor who had made millions building casinos in Las Vegas, and Dan Topping, who had inherited his money, MacPhail resigned in favor of longtime Yankees minor-league director George Weiss. A protégé of the departed Barrow, Weiss had a brilliant baseball mind but a charmless character; today he would be described as having poor people skills. He is often remembered as the dour penny-pincher who served as the villain of many of Mickey Mantle's favorite anecdotes about his ill treatment by the Yankees.

Following the 1948 season Weiss fired manager Bucky Harris. As conservative and stuffy as he was, however, there was never any doubt about Weiss's great administrative talents. That is why the entire baseball world was shocked when Weiss replaced Harris with a minor-league manager named Charles "Casey" Stengel. One reason was that the 59-year-old Stengel was nearing retirement age. Another was his undignified reputation as the National League's premiere clown; he had made a career out of his talent for goofy antics, hilarious double-talk, and enthusiastic partying. But the biggest reason that the move raised eyebrows was that Stengel was widely considered to be a loser.

Also known as "The Perfesser" for his rambling speeches to the press, Stengel got the nickname "Casey" from his habit of talking incessantly about his home town of Kansas City. Casey Stengel was a lifetime .284 hitter who played

*In February 1949, Casey Stengel gazes into a "crystal" ball to see what's in store for him during his first season as Yankees manager.*

14 years as a major-league outfielder, mostly with the Brooklyn Dodgers and the New York Giants of the 1910s. An excellent fielder with good speed and occasional power, Stengel the player in many ways resembled 1980s

and 1990s Mets and Phillies star Lenny Dykstra. Both men were strong, left-handed line-drive hitters and below average in height. Like Dykstra, Stengel tended to come through in clutch situations; he batted .393 with two home runs in twelve World Series games.

In his later years, as manager of the New York Yankees and the New York Mets, Stengel's sense of humor became legendary. One of his trademarks was Stengelese, an incomprehensible personal language that he would fall into when he did not want to answer a question—or purely for the fun of it. A few examples are:

- *Good pitching will always stop good hitting and vice versa.*
- *He's a remarkable catch, that Canzoneri [Chris Cannizzaro]. He's the only defensive catcher in baseball who can't catch.*
- *[To his barber] Shave and a haircut but don't cut my throat. I may want to do that myself.*
- *Now there's three things you can do in a base ball game: you can win or you can lose or it can rain.*
- *What the hell do I know? Most of the people my age are dead.*
- *[To a soldier who telephoned Stengel to second-guess a managerial move:] If you're so smart, let's see you get out of the army.*
- *There comes a time in every man's life, and I've had plenty of them.*

Stengel had retired in 1931 after six seasons in the minors as a player-manager. In 1934, like so many other protégés of John McGraw, he returned to the big leagues as a manager, running the Dodgers from 1934–36 and the Boston Braves from 1938–43. It was his performance with these two also-ran clubs that ruined Stengel's reputation as a baseball man almost beyond repair. In those nine seasons, Stengel produced only one winning season and finished fifth, sixth, or seventh in the eight-team NL every single year. In 1944 he was let go by the minor-league Milwaukee Brewers even though the team won the American Association pennant. Brewers owner Bill Veeck could have been speaking for all of baseball when he wrote: "Stengel is mentally a second-division major-leaguer. That is, he is entirely satisfied with a mediocre ball club as long as Stengel and his alleged wit are appreciated."

Even though he was always popular with most of the press, Stengel's image as a clown was so ingrained that it survived another minor-league championship, with the 1948 Oakland Oaks of the highly competitive Pacific Coast League. On the day that he was introduced to the press as the new manager of the 1949 New York Yankees by George Weiss, Stengel posed for a famous photo that shows him wearing pinstripes and gazing into a back lit baseball as though it were a crystal ball. "We have hired a clown," moaned one Yankees executive when he saw the picture. Yankee haters around the AL rejoiced. "Well, sirs and ladies," crowed Boston sportswriter Dave Egan, "the Yankees have now been mathematically eliminated from the 1949 pennant race. They eliminated themselves when they engaged Perfesser Casey Stengel to mismanage them for the next two years, and you may be sure that the perfesser will oblige to the best of his unique ability."

As it turned out, it was Weiss who was right and Dave Egan and the skeptics who were wrong. It is easy to forgive Egan when you consider what he did not know. In the fall of 1948, Edward "Whitey" Ford was an unknown pitcher going 16–8 in Norfolk of the Piedmont League in the low minors. Lawrence "Yogi" Berra had spent two seasons failing to win the Yankees starting catching job; many in the Yankee organization saw him as a defensive liability who might make it as a utility man or pinch hitter. Mickey Mantle was a high school football star in Commerce, Oklahoma, who appeared to have no future in pro sports after contracting osteomyelitis, a degenerative bone disease, from a football injury. The Yankees signed Mantle anyway. Within a few years, Weiss's farm system would bring Ford and Mantle to the point of superstardom. Recognizing Berra's potential, Stengel would turn him over to Yankees immortal Bill Dickey; under Dickey's instruction Berra would become the finest catcher in baseball. In various combinations, Casey Stengel, Whitey Ford, Yogi Berra, and Mickey Mantle forged a dynasty that dwarfs any other in baseball before or since, including the greatest of the great clubs of Babe Ruth, Lou Gehrig, or Joe DiMaggio. The Yankees of 1949 through 1964 won an incredible 14 of 16 AL pennants and become champions of the world nine times.

# THE YEAR: 1949

The National League treated its fans to another classic Brooklyn Dodgers–St. Louis Cardinals race that rivaled the thrillers of 1942 and 1946. The Cards were carried by their 28-year-old outfielder Stan Musial, who batted .338 (second only to batting champion Jackie Robinson), slugged .624, and collected 123 RBIs on 90 extra-base hits. With Jackie Robinson having his finest season the Dodgers were close to an even match with the Cards. The 30-year-old Robinson hit .342 with 12 triples and 16 homers; he led the NL in stolen bases with 37 and at the same time finished a surprising third in slugging percentage to Musial and Pittsburgh's Ralph Kiner. He was later voted NL MVP. Leading by a few games going into the final week of the season, the Cardinals lost four straight to give Brooklyn a chance to win the pennant by beating Philadelphia in the season finale. The Dodgers came through, downing the up-and-coming Phillies, 9-7, in a dramatic 10-inning contest.

The Phillies finished third with a lineup of talented 20-somethings that included 22-year-old shortstop Granville

"Granny" Hamner, 23-year-old third baseman Willie "Puddin' Head" Jones, and 22-year-old center fielder Richie Ashburn. The Pirates finished 12 games under .500 in sixth place, but Pittsburgh fans came out to see the slugging Kiner challenge Hack Wilson's NL home-run record. Kiner had his finest season in 1949, hitting 54 home runs, batting .310, and driving in 127 runs despite being walked a league-leading 117 times. The NL's top pitchers were Brooklyn's Preacher Roe, who went 15–6 with a 2.79 ERA; St. Louis's Howie Pollet, who went 20–9 with an ERA of 2.77 (second only to New York Giant Dave Koslo's 2.50); and the Boston Braves' ace Warren Spahn, who led the NL in wins and went 21–14 with a 3.07 ERA.

Ted Williams of the Boston Red Sox won his second MVP award in 1949, batting .343 with 150 runs, 159 RBIs, and 43 home runs. Barely nosed out for the batting title by Detroit's George Kell, Williams also led all AL hitters in on-base average at .490 and slugging at .650. The rest of the Boston offense improved around him. Center fielder Dom DiMaggio, shortstop Vern Stephens, and second baseman Johnny Pesky were third, fourth, and fifth in the AL in runs scored. Stephens tied Williams with 159 RBIs and was second in home runs with 39. Williams, DiMaggio, outfielder Al Zarilla, and Stephens were first, third, fourth, and fifth in doubles. The Red Sox won 96 games and scored the most runs in the major leagues, 896, but lost the pennant to Casey Stengel's New York Yankees.

None of the Yankees led the AL in any major hitting category. Other than shortstop Phil Rizzuto, who was second in the league in stolen bases with 18, only right fielder Tommy Henrich, third in homers with 24 and third-best in slugging percentage at .526, appeared in the top five. The club overcame injuries to the aging DiMaggio, Yogi Berra, and even late-season acquisition Johnny Mize. The pitching staff was reliable, if not spectacular, thanks to 21–10 Vic Raschi, 17–6 Allie Reynolds, 15–10 Eddie Lopat, and reliever Joe Page, who went 13–8 with 27 saves

*Warren Spahn warms up his pitching arm during spring training. The Braves' ace recorded eleven 20-win seasons in the 13 seasons between 1949 and 1961.*

and a 2.59 ERA in 60 appearances. No Yankee made the top three in ERA or wins.

For the first two games of the 1949 World Series the Dodgers and Yankees were like two heavyweight fighters feeling each other out. Reynolds won game one 1-0 and Preacher Roe evened things up in game two by the same score. Then the New Yorkers began to land telling blows, as Tommy Byrne and Joe Page overcame three Dodgers homers to take game three 4-3 on a three-run Yankee ninth; Lopat beat Newcombe 6-4 in game four; and Vic Raschi coasted to a 10-6 win in game five after the Yankees scored ten runs in the first six innings.

Amid all the disbelief from Yankee fans and gleeful predictions of doom from Yankee haters that greeted the hiring of Casey Stengel to manage the club in 1949, was this prophetic note that appeared in a wire-service story by a writer who had covered Stengel's championship season with the 1948 Oakland Oaks: "He'll bring a penchant for masterminding from the bench and a revolving door technique of substitutes that works like a charm." That one sentence pretty much sums up the Stengel managerial style. Going back to his playing days under John McGraw, Stengel had learned the value of left-right platooning—matching left-handers against right-handed pitchers on offense, and vice versa—a strategy that was much less common in 1930s and 1940s baseball than it is today. In fact, according to writer Robert Creamer, the term *platooning* was borrowed from football by New York sportswriter Harold Rosenthal to describe what Casey Stengel was doing with the 1949 Yankees.

Stengel's apprenticeship under McGraw, reinforced by more than 30 years of baseball experience, had also taught him the value of paying the closest possible attention to player matchups based on subtler factors, such as pitching and hitting styles, ballpark configurations, and human psychology. The greatest lesson Stengel learned from John McGraw was that of impatience: not to let players' established roles, a pitching rotation, or even concern for a player's health get in the way of success in the short term. Like his mentor McGraw and his protégé Billy Martin, Stengel's focus was always on winning today's game and worrying about tomorrow's game tomorrow. If that meant risking Whitey Ford's arm by pitching him on two days' rest or playing an injured Mickey Mantle when he should have been on the disabled list, then so be it. Obviously, this philosophy works best for a club with a deep farm system that can produce a steady stream of replacement talent. That was the beauty of the New York Yankees under Casey Stengel and George Weiss. Like a Pony Express courier in the Old West, Stengel used the whip and rode his clubs into the ground in a desperate, all-out effort to come in first. From 1949 through Stengel's firing by the Yankees in 1960, Weiss was always there to provide fresh horses.

Joe DiMaggio and the proud, veteran Yankees of 1949 were at first distinctly unenthusiastic about Stengel and his managerial philosophy. Fortunately for Stengel, however, circumstances prevented them from putting up much in the way of resistance. The 1949 Yankees had a deep, competent pitching staff of Allie Reynolds, Eddie Lopat, Vic Raschi, Fred Sanford, Tommy Byrne, and Joe Page. Only the 34-year-old Reynolds could have been called past his prime, and he had five good years left. Stengel left the pitching staff alone. It was a different story with the hitters. Outfielder Charlie Keller and second baseman George "Snuffy" Stirnweiss topped a list of big-name Yankee veterans who Stengel felt were at the end of the line.

Joe DiMaggio, who had not hidden his disdain for Stengel and his methods from reporters, discovered early in spring training that his surgically repaired right heel was far from healed. Unable to run, he would spend most of the 1949 season on the bench. Stengel was careful not to rock the Yankee boat; he always referred to DiMaggio, Keller, and Henrich as his "regular" outfielders, even as he gave more and more of their playing time to youngsters and substitutes, like Gene Woodling, Johnny Lindell, Cliff Mapes, and Hank Bauer.

In the infield, Stengel played veteran Phil Rizzuto every day, but he frequently substituted smooth-fielding young Jerry Coleman for Stirnweiss and platooned the right-handed Billy Johnson with veteran left-handed hitter Bobby Brown at third. At first base and catcher, two positions where there was no real established starter, Stengel could platoon, pinch-hit, and substitute to his heart's content. He used a long list of different players at one or both positions, including Norman "Babe" Young, Dick Kryhoski, Joe Collins, Gus Niarhos, Ralph Houk, Charlie Silvera, and Yogi Berra. Collins later said of Stengel:

> He would pinch-hit in situations that were ridiculous. He'd have two runs in, bases loaded, nobody out, and he'd pinch-hit Bauer for Woodling in the first inning when Woodling was on a hitting tear. And I'll be damned if Bauer didn't get a double or a triple about every time and, suddenly, we're ahead by five runs. Up in Boston [left-handed] Mel Parnell used to beat us every time we went there. So one day Casey came up with the idea he's going to put all left-handers in the lineup. From that time on, Mel Parnell never beat us one time. He couldn't pitch to left-handed hitters.[1]

Pitcher Eddie Lopat said: "They didn't have all those stats [then] that they have today. [Stengel] had a wonderful memory. He didn't have to whip out the stat sheets and read data. He had it on his fingertips. That was one of his big assets." Stengel's unorthodox system worked wonders in 1949, even though the team was so riddled by injuries that only one player, the steady shortstop Phil Rizzuto, appeared in more than 122 games at one position. Veteran outfielder Tommy Henrich batted .287 with 24 home runs in only 115 games. Yogi Berra hit 20 homers in 116 games. The injuries, combined with Stengel's system, meant that few Yankees appeared on the offensive leader boards, but the club as a whole produced. Part-time outfielders Hank Bauer, Johnny Lindell, Cliff Mapes, Gene Woodling, and Joe DiMaggio combined for 42 homers and 221 RBIs. As a team, New York scored 829 runs, second in the AL only to the Red Sox.

Stengel's managing, the club's solid pitching, and the

brilliant play of his youthful corps of subs kept the Yankees in the pennant hunt through the first half of the season despite an awesome five-month display of offense put on by Ted Williams and the Boston Red Sox. Most amazing of all was that the Yankees' biggest star, Joe DiMaggio, had not appeared in any of the season's first 65 games. Then, one day in late June, DiMaggio got out of bed in his New York hotel room and felt something unfamiliar—no pain. For the first time since mid-season 1948 his right heel finally felt well. Two days later, fitted with a special spikeless cushioned shoe, he started his first game of the season, game one of a three-game series in Boston's Fenway Park.

DiMaggio would later call this series "the most satisfying three days of my life." Just as he had so many times when he was young and healthy, Joe DiMaggio stepped into the Yankee lineup and took over the game and the series. He beat Boston with a two-run homer in his second at bat of game one. He launched a Yankee comeback in game two with a three-run homer in the fifth with Boston leading 7-1; he won the game with another home run in the eighth. With the Yankees leading 3-2 in the seventh inning of game three, DiMaggio put the game away with a three-run home run off Boston ace Parnell. He finished the series with five hits, four of them out of the park.

DiMaggio carried the Yankees for the next two months, but nothing was destined to come easy for the 1949 Yankees. When Joe DiMaggio was knocked out of action by a serious case of pneumonia in September, Joe McCarthy's club roared back into first place. The race for the AL pennant came down to two season-ending games between the Yankees and the Red Sox in New York. Boston held a one-game lead. That meant that all the Red Sox had to do to win the pennant was to win one of the two games; the Yankees had to sweep or finish second. Weak and still feverish, DiMaggio insisted on playing both games. He contributed a single and a double as the Yankees won the first game, 5-4, behind Allie Reynolds and Joe Page. In the second game, an exhausted DiMaggio removed himself in the ninth when he misplayed a deep fly ball to center by Bobby Doerr into a two-run triple. New York held on, however, to win 5-3 on Jerry Coleman's three-run eighth-inning double and fine pitching by Vic Raschi. For the Yankees, it was the sixteenth first-place finish in their history; for Stengel it was his first and sweetest big-league pennant as a manager. "I want to thank all these players," he announced during an emotional postgame locker-room celebration, "for giving me the greatest thrill of my life."

*Casey Stengel and the rest of the Yankees whoop it up after winning the 1949 AL pennant. They had just beaten the Red Sox to earn a trip to the World Series.*

As George Weiss methodically rebuilt the Yankees of Joe DiMaggio into the dynasty of the 1950s and 1960s, the hiring of Casey Stengel and his reshaping of the 1949 team was only the beginning. The second and third pieces of the puzzle came in 1950 in the form of an awkward, left-handed hitting catcher and outfielder named Yogi Berra, and a young left-handed pitcher from Queens in New York City named Whitey Ford.

Discovered by the Yankees in the same working-class Italian section of St. Louis that produced NL catcher Joe Garagiola, by 1950 Berra had become a problem for the Yankees. Even though his hitting skills were obvious—he had torn up minor-league pitching and established himself as a big-league hitter with 34 homers and 189 RBIs in 1949 and 1950 combined—Berra was a disaster with the glove. "He had trouble when he first came up throwing runners out," said pitcher Eddie Lopat. "He had a good arm but he didn't know how to get in position to throw. He was terrible in blocking balls, throwing runners out, and we had a tough time winning." Some were ready to give up and make Berra an outfielder, but Casey Stengel disagreed. He turned Berra over to coach and Hall of Fame ex-catcher Bill Dickey, who spent most of the 1949 season, as Berra put it, "learning me his experiences." As America would soon find out, Berra had a goofy verbal style of his own that rivaled the finest Stengelese. Dickey later remembered, "The Yankee staff would hold a meeting every week and talk about the club, and every week they'd ask me, 'You gonna make a catcher out of Berra?' And I kept putting them off because I hadn't seen enough of him. Finally, I gave them their answer: 'I think he ought to make a pretty good catcher.'" The events of the next decade proved this to be one of the great understatements in baseball history. Yogi Berra won the regular catching job for good in 1950 and hit .322 with 28 home runs and 124 RBIs. He went on to hit .285 lifetime with 358 career homers.

Berra's defense improved from fair to excellent to simply amazing. Yankee pitchers from those days still tell stories of how Berra would decide in a split second to drop a foul tip because he had seen that an opposing base runner had gotten a good jump and was on his way to stealing second on the pitch—or the times that he turned an attempted suicide squeeze bunt into an unassisted double play by grabbing the bunt in fair territory, tagging the batter, and then diving back to tag the baserunner sliding in from third. (Think about the quickness involved in that one.)

Berra was a notorious bad ball hitter at the plate and generally appeared awkward. Like the immortal Honus Wagner—and, to some extent, Casey Stengel—Berra's image as a comedian continues to obscure the memory of his greatness on the baseball field. Berra's answer to Wagner's corny stories and Stengel's incoherent ramblings was his famous malaprops. Even though it is true that people have embellished and added to them over the years—as he himself observed in classic style, "I didn't say everything I said"—a good 25 percent to 50 percent of known Berra-isms seem to be genuinely from the Yogi's mouth. Some of the best loved include:

- *You can observe a lot by watching.*
- *It's never over 'till it's over.*
- *How the hell are you gonna think and hit at the same time?*
- *It's déjà vu all over again.*
- *[About a restaurant] Nobody goes there any more. It's too crowded.*
- *If you come to a fork in the road, take it.*
- *If people don't want to come out to the park, nobody's going to stop them.*

Whatever corner of Berra's brain produced sayings like these, there was never any doubting his tremendous baseball intelligence and shrewdness. Berra and Stengel formed a team within the Yankees team that had a lot to do with the club's trademark heads-up style of play. "I guess Yogi was Casey's favorite," Billy Johnson remembered, "his assistant manager." It is worth noting that the two were all business when it came to the game on the field. "Casey never talked that way to me," Berra once said, referring to Stengelese, "but then again, I was handling his pitchers."

By the early 1950s, Yogi Berra had finished third in one MVP balloting and first in another, and his hitting and defense were approaching the level that Yankee fans began to debate the question of who was the better catcher, Berra or his mentor, Bill Dickey. Then came 1954 and 1955, when Berra caught 294 games, batted .307 and .272, hit 49 homers and drove in 233 runs. He was voted AL MVP both years. Berra was now certifiably out of Dickey's league. While Dickey never won an MVP award, despite his impressive offensive numbers, Berra had won the award three times. Even more impressively, he also finished second once, third once, and fourth once. In the heart of his career, from 1950 through 1956, Berra never finished out of the top five in the MVP balloting. From 1948 until 1961 he never once failed to receive at least one MVP vote. Consider that this was in spite of playing on a team studded with all-time greats and perennial all-stars like Phil Rizzuto, Tommy Henrich, Joe Page, Allie Reynolds, Vic Raschi, Mickey Mantle, Roger Maris, and Whitey Ford. There were times in Bill Dickey's career when he was considered the best, or one of the best, catchers in the AL. For the middle ten years of Yogi Berra's career, however, the question was whether he was the best, or one of the best, *players* in the AL.

# THE YEAR: 1950

The NL flag was taken by one of the most obscure underdogs in pennant-race history, the 1950 Philadelphia

Phillies. This is a team so little-remembered today that it would take a trivia champion to name more than four or five of the Phillies starters. Nicknamed the "Whiz Kids," the young Phillies had jumped from sixth to third place in 1949 before edging out Brooklyn for the 1950 pennant in the final inning of the final game of the season. After lead-off man Richie Ashburn, who was probably the only great everyday player on the team, the Philadelphia attack depended on power hitters Del Ennis, Puddin' Head Jones, and Andy Seminick. Ennis led the NL in RBIs; Ashburn led in triples. The team's thin pitching staff was carried by starters Robin Roberts and Curt Simmons, with the help of heroic super reliever Jim Konstanty, who won the NL MVP award thanks to his 16 wins and 22 saves in an amazing 74 appearances. St. Louis's Stan Musial won the fourth of his seven NL batting titles, hitting .346 to beat out Brooklyn's Jackie Robinson at .328. Pittsburgh's Ralph Kiner won his fifth consecutive home run title with 47. Warren Spahn and Johnny Sain of Boston combined for 41 wins; Giant and Cardinal Jim Hearn took the ERA title at 1.94, beating out New York's head-hunting Sal Maglie at 2.71 and Cincinnati's fearsome sidearmer Ewell "The Whip" Blackwell at 2.97.

The 1950 New York Yankees, featuring a Stengelesque blend of old and new, won the AL pennant by a fairly narrow margin over Detroit, Boston, and Cleveland. Veterans Joe DiMaggio and Phil Rizzuto had good years—Rizzuto hit .324 and was voted AL MVP—and Johnny Mize produced 25 homers and 72 RBIs in only 274 at bats. Youngsters Collins, Coleman, Johnson, Bauer, Woodling, and Berra played regularly and well. Bolstered by the mid-season call-up of Whitey Ford, a young left-hander who went 9–1 with a 2.81 ERA, the solid pitching staff of Raschi, Reynolds, Lopat, Byrne, and Page allowed the second-fewest runs in the AL. Even without Ted Williams, who suffered an elbow injury in the All-Star game, the Red Sox put on their usual impressive offensive show. Billy Goodman

won the batting title at .354; Vern Stephens won the RBI
title with 144; and the names of Red Sox Walt Dropo,
Dom DiMaggio, Al Zarilla, Johnny Pesky, and Bobby
Doerr peppered the leader boards in various hitting categories. The Tigers' George Kell was the batting title runner-
up at .340, and Cleveland's Al Rosen led the AL in homers
with 37. In Philadelphia, Jimmy Dykes was named manager after owner-manager Connie Mack finally retired at the
age of 87 after 50 straight seasons at the helm of the Athletics. Mack finished first nine times, last seventeen times,
and still holds the all-time records for most games managed, 7,878; he won more games and lost more games
than any manager before or since.

The 1950 World Series was an unmitigated disaster for
the Phillies, who entered the series with their number one
pitcher, Roberts, exhausted and their number two, Simmons, drafted into the army and unavailable. The powerful
Yankees swept Philadelphia with one hand tied behind
their backs. After Raschi outdueled Konstanty, 1-0, in game
one, the Yankees took the next three games, 2-1, 3-2, and
5-2, despite batting a mere .222 with only 2 home runs.
"In another five years," boasted George Weiss, "they'll
appreciate how good this team really is."

A rookie sensation in 1950, Whitey Ford lost the next two
seasons to military service. When he returned in 1953, he
stepped into the Yankees pitching rotation and instantly
established himself as the ace, going 18–6 with an ERA of
3.00 followed by seasons of 16–8, 18–7, 19–6, 11–5,
14–7, 16–10, 12–9, 25–4, 17–8, 24–7, and 17–6. By the
time he retired in 1967, Ford had won two ERA titles and
compiled a career won-lost record of 236–106 with an
ERA of 2.75. His .690 winning percentage is the third-best
of all time—the best ever for a pitcher with 200 wins—and
he holds World Series marks for most wins, ten; most
games, 22; and most innings pitched, 146. Physically on
the small side and lacking an overpowering fastball, the

easygoing Ford won with intelligence, control, and dura-bility—mixed with a little gamesmanship. His specialty was doctoring the ball with a variety of substances, including plain old dirt. Umpire Bill Kinnamon remembered with admiration Ford's ability to turn a brand-new baseball into a filthy, misshapen lump :

*Once, after I told [Yankees second baseman] Bobby Richardson that I didn't think there was another human being on earth who could get a ball dirtier than Whitey Ford, Bobby looked at me and said, "You know, I've been playing with him a long time, and I don't really know how he does it myself. Just about the time I think I know exactly what he's doing, he'll change and do something else.*[2]

The 1951 season saw the retirement of Joe DiMaggio, the last link to the great Yankee teams of the Joe McCarthy era. But that was also the year that George Weiss and the great Yankees system provided Casey Stengel with a player who represented the finishing touch on the greatest Yankee dynasty of them all—Mickey Mantle. Mantle arrived in 1951 as a nervous, bumbling Class D shortstop with more speed and more power than most baseball men had ever seen. A switch-hitter who hit long balls so far that the Yankees began to measure them as a publicity stunt—this is the origin of the term "tape measure shot"—Mantle gave the Yankees of the Stengel era the missing ingredients of dominating home-run power and a superstar to make the fans forget DiMaggio and to rival Ruth and Gehrig. As DiMaggio faded in the late 1940s, the Yankees had begun to lose the monopoly on home-run hitting that had earned previous clubs nicknames like "Murderers' Row" and the "Bronx Bombers." This was important not only because of Yankee history, but because offensive baseball in the 1950s was all about power. An historic low point in the use of the running game, the 1950s was sort of a return to the 1930s without the interesting characters or the gaudy batting averages. As baseball historian Bill James writes:

> In the early part of the 50s, every team approached the game with the same essential philosophy: get people on base and hit home runs. Every team, whether one of the best or one of the worst, featured players in the class of Gus Zernial, Ralph Kiner, Hank Sauer, Roy Sievers, Jim Lemon, Luke Easter, Eddie Robinson, Bob Niemann, Gus Triandos, Vic Wertz, Bobby Thomson, Roy Campanella, Sid Gordon, Willie Jones, Rocky Colavito, and Ted Kluszewski, muscular men not long on grace nor noted for acceleration, but men who commanded large salaries by their proficiency at the art of long hitting.[3]

In 1949 and 1950, the New York Yankees finished third in the AL in team home runs, outdone by both the Red Sox of Williams, Stephens, and Dropo and the Cleveland Indians of Al Rosen and Larry Doby. With the arrival of future 500 home run–man Mantle, however, along with an ever-more-powerful supporting cast made up of players like Berra, Bauer, Woodling, Bill "Moose" Skowron, Roger Maris, and Elston Howard, Stengel's clubs reasserted the Yankees' traditional mastery of the home run. As the 1950s gave way to the 1960s, although Detroit and Boston put up good power numbers—helped, of course, by playing in small, 1910s-era ballparks—the AL home run leader board was dominated by the Yankees, who finished first in team homers in 1951, 1955, 1956, 1958, 1960, and 1961. Only the Cleveland Indians of Rosen, Doby, Wertz, and Colavito could rival New York's awesome and consistent delivery of the big fly. The 1961 Yankees were the greatest sluggers of all. With seven players in double figures in home runs and two hitting over 50, that team produced a total of 240 home runs, setting a record that stood until the notorious home run explosion of 1996.

The organizational brilliance of George Weiss, the money of Dan Topping and Del Webb, the restless creativity of Casey Stengel, the strength and intelligence of Yogi Berra, the caginess and poise of Whitey Ford, and the raw power of Mickey Mantle—all of these combined to make the New York Yankees of 1949 through 1964 the baseball dynasty to end all baseball dynasties. On the field, there was nothing like them. The Yankees of 1949 through 1953 won five straight world championships, in the process winning 20 and losing only 8 World Series games. That had never been done before—not by the clubs of Ruth, Gehrig, or DiMaggio—and it has not been approached since. These five champions bore the unmistakable Stengel imprint. Pitcher Eddie Lopat remembered:

> *In those five years, 96 players went through the club. People say how can you win a pennant five years in a row with 96 players going through a club. Well, the nucleus was there the whole time and they just filled in around it where they needed. Actually of the five World Series we won there were only 12 [sic] of us who were on that club through it all: Berra, Joe Collins, Rizzuto, Gene Woodling, Hank Bauer, Raschi, Reynolds, and myself, and Charlie Silvera.[4]*

The Yankees appeared in 14 of the 16 World Series played between 1949 and 1964 and won 9 of them. There is an old saying that a man can be judged by the quality of his enemies. If you apply this standard to baseball teams, then the greatness of New York Yankees of this era is further magnified. Both non-Yankee AL pennant-winners of the 1950s were great clubs managed by the immortal Al

*Yogi Berra embraces Whitey Ford during a locker-room victory celebration. The catcher and pitcher were part of the Yankees' dynasty that won the World Series in 1949, 1950, 1951, 1952, 1953, 1956, 1958, 1961, 1962. (Ford did not play in the 1949, 1951, or 1952 World Series.)*

Lopez. His 1954 AL champions, the Cleveland Indians, had one of the finest clubs in AL history. They left a top-notch Yankee club in the dust, even though New York won

103 games—the most victories ever by any of Stengel's teams. Armed with batting champion Bobby Avila, slugging third baseman Al Rosen, and home run and RBI leader Larry Doby, Lopez's Indians also boasted one of the greatest pitching staffs ever. Early Wynn went 23–11 that year with an ERA of 2.73; Bob Lemon went 23–7 with a 2.72 ERA; Mike Garcia went 19–8 and won the AL ERA title at 2.64; and veteran Bob Feller turned in a 13–3 season. Believe it or not, the Cleveland staff went even deeper than that. Art Houtteman won 15 and lost 7; Hal Newhouser went 7–2 with a 2.51 ERA; and Don Moss and Ray Narleski had terrific seasons in relief by the standards of the day, winning 9 and saving 20 between them.

As for their World Series opponents, the Yankees faced Brooklyn's NL dynasty five times and lost only once, in a close, seven-game series in 1955. The Dodgers of the late 1940s and 1950s featured an all-Hall-of-Fame lineup that included sluggers Duke Snider, Gil Hodges, and Roy Campanella, and multiple-threat players like Jackie Robinson and Pee Wee Reese. Their pitching staffs were studded with stars such as Don Newcombe, Carl Erskine, Johnny Podres, Preacher Roe, and Joe Black. Don Drysdale and Sandy Koufax came along just before the team moved to Los Angeles, where the Dodgers continued to win.

Success on this scale bred a special attitude into the New York Yankees. Or perhaps it was the attitude that led to all the winning. As one-time Yankee Bob Cerv put it:

> *It's the character of the players that makes a winner. I was on other clubs. Hell, I could never understand how they could beat someone 14-1, then lose for the next three or four days resting on their laurels. They'd fatten up their average. They could coast. The Yanks never worked that way. They played just as hard as they could every day. When we crossed that white line we went to work. We'd always say: "Well, let's go to work!" And boy did we!*[5]

Many opponents saw the Yankee attitude as something closer to arrogance. Either way, the unbeatable Yankees of the postwar era came to symbolize the spirit and the experience of an entire nation. World War II had left the economy of most industrialized nations in a shambles. The big exception was the United States, whose unbombed factories and relatively untouched people had created a mighty, efficient war machine that was ready to retool and become a peacetime industrial juggernaut. Like Stengel's Yankees, the American economy bounced back from the war years and gathered momentum throughout the 1950s until it seemed to operate at an almost unfair advantage. Like Mantle going all out for the home run on every swing, by virtue of its sheer power it rolled over all comers and kept going until it ran up the score. Americans sold their cars, tractors, wheat, plastic, steel, oil, and aluminum in amazing quantities, unchallenged by foreign competitors, in every corner of the globe.

Wealth poured into the U.S., creating thousands of millionaires, sending millions of former soldiers to college, financing the construction of vast suburban housing developments, and creating a class of unionized blue-collar workers who lived lives of material comfort that put the rich of many other nations to shame. Like Stengel's Yankees, America was now the world's overdog. And rooting for the Yankees, as the popular expression of the time went, was like rooting for that symbol of American corporate might, U.S. Steel.

Even though there was a dark side to baseball in the 1949–64 era, just as there was to American life in general, fans' memories of those days remain rosy and positive. We remember the alleged innocence and prosperity of suburban life in the 1950s and forget its stifling conformity and intolerance, as well as negative by-products of suburbanization, such as white flight from large cities and the creation or expansion of vast inner-city ghettoes that persist to this day. African-Americans were largely excluded from the suburban dream and were never more invisible culturally than in the 1950s. Popular entertainment of the racist 1910s and 1920s may not have treated African-Americans with humanity or respect, but at least African-American characters and plot elements made an occasional appearance. A visitor from Mars who watched every episode of such popular TV sitcoms as *The Donna Reed Show, Leave It to Beaver,* or *The Andy Griffith Show* would never know that Americans of African descent even existed.

We prefer to idolize Mickey Mantle and refuse to see the perpetual adolescent, ill-mannered alcoholic, and wretched father and husband that he so obviously was. Many fans even take Mantle's drinking, womanizing, and stubborn refusal to take care of his body and turn them around into a form of martyrdom. The America of the 1950s loved a winner and nobody won more than the New York Yankees.

While it was happening, the Yankees' dominance of baseball became an accepted fact of life, inspiring the popular 1957 musical *Damn Yankees,* a fantasy whose premise is that supernatural forces are required to give another team a shot at the AL flag. As the 1960s came along and the Yankees remained as unbeatable as ever, some Americans resented the team's success and revived the ancient call to "break up" the club. Most, however, were content to identify with the Yankees' success and happily rooted for Mickey Mantle, whose fair hair, unassuming manner, and amazing success were fast transforming him into a crew-cut, All-American god.

As the memory of World War II faded, the economy boomed, and it seemed as though everyone from milkmen to machinists to corporate middle managers would all get their chance at the new, modern suburban lifestyle—complete with television, automobile, and weekend cocktails around the backyard pool—most

Americans felt like winners. Thanks to the aura of Mantle, the team's amazing record of success, and, not least, the fact that fans could now watch postseason games on television, the New York Yankees of 1949–64 became America's team to an extent that the NFL Dallas Cowboys of the 1980s or the NL Atlanta Braves of the early 1990s could only dream of.

# CHAPTER TWO

# "What a Shot!" Mickey Mantle Swings for the Fences

Baseball talent scouting is much more organized today than it was in the old days. First, there are no secrets. Every scout on every major-league team has access to a vast, computerized database of prospects; virtually anybody who ever played well for more than a week or two at the high school, American Legion, or college level has been scouted and reported on. Second, except for foreign-born prospects, there is no competition to sign players because of the amateur draft. The way the draft works is that every June teams take turns, in reverse order of how they finished in the previous major-league season, picking players they want to sign. According to the rules of organized baseball, no team can try to sign a player drafted by another team for a fixed length of time. The effect of the draft is that the cost of amateur talent is held down and that talent is more or less evenly distributed among the professional teams.

In the 1940s and 1950s, however, there was no draft system at all. The teams with the best and the most scouts—and the most money—took the lion's share of the nation's prospects. The haphazard nature of scouting in the early days also meant that every once in a while a great player could be overlooked and then truly be discovered by a particularly discerning or lucky scout, something that is virtually unheard of, at least in the United States, today. One famous example is Yankee scout Paul Krichell's discovery of Lou Gehrig in 1923. Watching a ball game at Columbia University's South Field, Krichell saw the square-shouldered Columbia pitcher smack a home run that cleared the outfield fence and traveled 450 feet in the air all the way to 116th Street and Broadway. From that one swing, Krichell's scout's eye could visualize Gehrig's whole, glorious future as a home run hitter. "I knew then" he later said, "that I'd never have another moment like it the rest of my life."

Twenty-five years later, another Yankee scout, Tom Greenwade, had an experience that, as he put it, gave him an idea of "how Paul Krichell felt when he first saw Lou Gehrig." Greenwade had been sent to Oklahoma to watch a teenaged Mickey Mantle play baseball. Mantle was very fast, and he had attracted more attention as a football prospect than as a baseball prospect, but a seriously infected leg wound had scared off most scouts from both sports. There was even talk of Mantle undergoing an amputation. As Greenwade told the story:

*He looked kind of small—he hadn't filled out yet— and I just didn't recognize how coordinated he was. I didn't know he was a switch-hitter! In [the first] two games [Greenwade had seen Mantle] he had only batted left-handed, because he was facing all right-handed pitchers. In the third game, against a left-handed pitcher, he stepped into the batter's box from the right side, and I didn't know what to make of it. Mickey's father was sitting right next to me and I asked him how long his boy had been a switch-hitter. He said: "Since he was about eight." Then I looked again at Mickey, and he pulled a line-shot to left for a double, and it all came togeth-*

*er. Finally I could see that seventeen-year-old body, how it worked like a damn baseball machine, and how it was gonna fill out. I understood how he'd been blessed. And I was blessed, too.*[1]

Greenwade offered Mickey Mantle a minor-league contract with a signing bonus of $1,400. The dirt-poor son of a frustrated amateur ballplayer who worked six days a week in a lead mine to support his family, Mantle signed. Two years later, Mickey Mantle had fulfilled much of Tom Greenwade's vision. Thanks to penicillin, a newly invented antibiotic, his leg was saved. Mantle had grown bigger and stronger, and he had cut through the minors like a hot knife through butter. After batting .383 with 68 extra-base hits for Joplin in the Western Association, Mantle found himself in 1951 working out in spring training with the world champion Yankees. It would all have been a bit dizzying, even if Casey Stengel were not telling every reporter in sight that his prize rookie was "the next Babe Ruth, Lou Gehrig, and Joe DiMaggio all rolled into one."

The next chapter in the Mickey Mantle legend is not the most glorious. After a hot start with the Yankees in 1951, the young shortstop-turned-outfielder fell flat on his face. His batting average dropped from .308 to .261 in less than two months. After striking out five straight times in a Memorial Day doubleheader against Boston, Mantle was sent down to the Yankees' top minor-league club in Kansas City. The Yankees tried not to hurt their young star's confidence. When asked by a reporter if Mantle was through, Casey Stengel snarled: "You wish you were through like that kid's through." Stengel explained that Mantle was only being sent down for a limited time, in order to snap him out of his slump.

Mantle did not listen; he was only 19 years old, but he felt like a failure. He descended into self-pity and, as he recalled, "didn't get a hit for, like, 22 times at bat." He telephoned his father and told him that he wanted to quit baseball for good. Four hours later, Elvin Mantle showed up at his son's hotel room; he had driven straight from Commerce, Oklahoma. As Mantle later told the story, "I thought he'd come up and pat me on the back and start saying, 'Hey, hang in there' or something like that. Instead, he really let me have it for about five minutes, calling me a coward and a quitter." The elder Mantle started packing Mickey's bags, telling him that it was time to forget baseball, come home, and get a job in the mines.

When he recovered from the shock, Mickey Mantle got the message his father was trying to give him: it was time to grow up and live up to his talent. He broke out of his slump, hit .361 with 11 home runs for Kansas City, and fought his way back up to the big club in September. Mantle's recovery came not a moment too soon.

The 1951 season may have been the first for Mickey Mantle, but it turned out to be the last for another future Hall of Famer, Joe DiMaggio. That year DiMaggio batted only .263 with 12 homers and 71 RBIs as his 36-year-old body quit on him. Racked by pain in his heels, knees, and throwing shoulder, the proud DiMaggio turned down a $100,000 contract for 1952, saying, "Old injuries caught up with me and brought on new ones. I found that it was hard for me to straighten up after I picked up a ground ball. All the fun had gone out of playing the game." Joe DiMaggio had started his career as another in a long line of Yankee outfielders who failed to make the New York fans forget Babe Ruth—he was regularly booed during the early years for his youthful mistakes, his frequent minor injuries, and his infamous contract holdouts—but ended it as the object of fervent hero worship that approached that inspired by the Babe.

As the years have passed since he retired, DiMaggio has, if anything, grown in stature. Fed in part by the mystery and dignity of his off-field life, including his ill-fated marriage to film sex symbol Marilyn Monroe and his steadfast unwillingness to cooperate with would-be biographers,

*On April 14, 1951, Casey Stengel gives his prize rookie,
Mickey Mantle, instructions prior to a Yankees-Dodgers
exhibition game at Ebbets Field.*

the DiMaggio aura has retained its magic. Still, he will always be remembered foremost for the polished beauty of his game and for the selfless, total dedication to winning he demonstrated every time he set foot on a professional baseball diamond. As Red Smith wrote:

> If he were not such a matchless craftsman, he might be a more spectacular player and so more highly regarded. But you don't rate a great ballplayer according to his separate special talents. You must rank him off the sum total of his component parts, and on this basis there has not been during Joe's big-league existence, a rival close to him. None other in his time has combined such savvy and fielding and hitting and throwing.

## THE YEAR: 1951

Overcoming a shaky start by Mickey Mantle and a shaky finish by Joe DiMaggio, Casey Stengel won one of the quietest of his ten Yankee pennants. New York pitching was dominating, thanks to 21-game-winners Eddie Lopat and Vic Raschi, and Allie Reynolds, who threw two no-hitters, the second in the pennant-clinching game. Hitting .294 with 27 home runs, Yogi Berra was voted MVP on a club that coolly pulled away from rivals Cleveland and Boston in the final month of the season. Philadelphia's Ferris Fain won the batting title at .344; Orestes "Minnie" Minoso of Cleveland and Chicago was second at .326. Playing for the White Sox and A's, Gus Zernial led the AL in homers with 33 and RBIs with 129. Yet another traded player, White Sox-turned-Tigers pitcher Saul Rogovin, took the AL ERA title at 2.78. The weirdest event of the year, at least in the AL, occurred on August 19, when St. Louis Browns owner Bill Veeck sent in midget Eddie Gaedel to pinch-hit in a situation in which the Browns needed a base runner. Attired in a tiny Browns uniform with the number 1/8 stitched onto his jersey, Gaedel took advantage of his three-inch-high strike zone to draw a walk on four pitches. He trotted down to first amid gales of laughter from the stands, and was then pinch-run for by a real player. Organized baseball was not amused. Gaedel's contract was voided the next day by AL president Will Harridge on the grounds that Gaedel had made a farce of the game. "What about Ted Williams?" protested former St. Louis manager Luke Sewell. "When I was running the Browns and had to face the Red Sox, Williams made a farce of almost every game there was."

The race for the NL flag between the New York Giants and the Brooklyn Dodgers featured the greatest baseball comeback since the 1914 "Miracle" Braves. For a while, it was not even a race; on August 11 Leo Durocher's Giants had fallen 13½ games off the pace. Even after reeling off a 16-game winning streak, the Giants were still 6 games behind Brooklyn. But the Giants kept chipping away at the Dodgers' lead until the two teams finished the regular season in a dead heat. Finally, Bobby Thomson's ninth-inning, score-reversing homer in playoff game number three made the Giants one of baseball history's unlikeliest champions.

The NL leader boards of 1951 were monopolized by the Dodgers and Giants. Stan Musial beat out Richie Ashburn to win another batting title with an average of .355, but Brooklyn's Jackie Robinson and Roy Campanella came in third and fourth, and New York's Monte Irvin finished fifth. After perennial home run champ Ralph Kiner of Pittsburgh, the NL home run leaders were Gil Hodges, Campanella, and Bobby Thomson. Irvin led the NL in RBIs with 121. On the pitching side, Dodger Preacher Roe, Giant Sal Maglie, Dodger Don Newcombe, Giant Larry Jansen, and Giant Jim Hearn formed the top five in winning percentage. Maglie was nosed out by one-season wonder Chet Nichols of Boston for the ERA title, 2.93 to 2.88. The MVP voting was more of the same. Musial, who finished second to Campanella, was the only player in the top six who did not play his home games in New York City.

Mickey Mantle hit .311 with 23 homers and 87 RBIs in 1952 and .295 with 21 homers and 92 RBIs the season after that. From 1954 through 1961, however, Mantle took his game up to the level of the all-time great sluggers in baseball history. Over those eight seasons, the soft-spoken young man with the broad, easy smile led the AL in runs six times, bases on balls four times, and home runs four times. His homer totals—27, 37, 52, 34, 42, 31, 40, and 54—could have come from the middle of Babe Ruth's career. Mantle had something else in common with the Babe; he went for the fences with almost every swing, no matter whether the team needed a three-run home run or a bunt single. As teammate Joe Collins put it, "Mickey tried to hit every one like they don't count under four hundred feet." For a while, this caused tension between Stengel and the young slugger, whom the manager saw as his personal gift from the baseball gods.

Seeing a younger version of himself, but blessed with much more power and the ability to switch-hit, Stengel wanted Mickey to steal bases, play perfect defense, and become an all-around offensive and defensive threat, but playing the percentages did not seem to be in Mantle's nature. Billy Martin once told the story of seeing Stengel blow up at Mantle for trying to hit a pitch out of the park in a situation that called for shortening his swing and making contact: "I saw the old man grab Mickey by the back of the neck and shake him hard. He said, 'Don't let me see you do that again, you little bastard!'"

Like other heroes of his generation, Mantle played the rebel without a cause—the teenager who defies authority and its values without any real values of his own to assert in their place. Even though Mickey Mantle developed into one of the greatest hitters ever by doing things his way,

Stengel never entirely got over his disappointment with Mantle for not playing smarter or taking better care of himself. Years later, when reporters would ask Stengel to name his personal all-time all-star team, he never included Mickey Mantle.

# THE YEAR: 1952

The idea that the New York Yankees were favored to win the pennant every year during Casey Stengel's time as manager is a creation of hindsight. While that may have been true in the late 1950s and early 1960s, Stengel's first half-dozen Yankees teams were frequently picked to finish second or even third. The 1952 season is a good example. That year, reporters looked at Cleveland's slugging offense of Luke Easter, Larry Doby, and Al Rosen; and the team's daunting pitching staff of Early Wynn, Mike Garcia, Bob Lemon, and Bob Feller, and named them the prohibitive favorites to win the AL flag. As for the Yankees, they had lost DiMaggio to old age and were about to lose second baseman Jerry Coleman and pitcher Whitey Ford to the military draft. Stengel, however, put his protégé Billy Martin in at second; got good seasons out of aging starting pitchers Allie Reynolds, Vic Raschi, Johnny Sain, and Ed Lopat—average age almost 35; and won 95 games and the pennant. The Yankees took a hard-fought World Series from Brooklyn, four games to three.

Philadelphia's Ferris Fain won a second batting title at .327. Indians Doby and Easter were one and two in homers, with 32 and 31; and Al Rosen led the AL in RBIs with 105. Philadelphia's Bobby Shantz was the MVP in the AL, going 24–7 with a 2.48 ERA, third-best in the AL behind Reynolds's 2.06 and Garcia's 2.37.

In the NL, Brooklyn avenged 1951 by winning the pennant by 4½ games over an archrival New York club that lost Willie Mays for most of the year to the military draft. Five Dodger pitchers won in double figures, including Carl

Erskine, Preacher Roe, Billy Loes, Ben Wade, and rookie sensation Joe Black, who went 15–4 with 15 saves and an ERA of 2.15. Chicago's Hank Sauer won the MVP. Braves slugger Eddie Mathews won the home run title with 47; Brooklyn's Carl Furillo led in batting at .344; and Dodger catcher Campanella led the NL in RBIs with 142. Milwaukee Braves star Warren Spahn won the ERA title at 2.10 and led in wins with 23.

One of Stengel's biggest worries was Mantle's increasing interest in drinking and carousing. Together with second baseman Billy Martin, a fiery player who had starred on Stengel's pennant-winning Oakland Oaks club, and Whitey Ford, Mantle formed a celebrated "rat pack" that mimicked the famous Las Vegas rat pack of entertainers Frank Sinatra, Dean Martin, Sammy Davis Jr., and others. Life for the Yankees stars became one year-long party after another, interrupted only for a few hours each day by a baseball game. It was one thing for a player who appeared only every fifth day or for a bottom of the order hitter to behave like this, but Stengel began to worry that one day Mantle would leave his game for good in some bar or night club. The manager called Ford, Martin, and Mantle into his office and asked them, "Do you know who King Solomon was?" When they shook their heads, Stengel launched into the following parable from the Book of Casey:

> Well, King Solomon was a guy that had a hundred wives, and they couldn't all live in the same house with him, so they had to be scattered all around town. But if he's got all these wives, he couldn't go get 'em, so he had a guy that lived with him would run and get the wives and bring 'em to him if he wanted one. Even if he had one way across town that he wanted, this guy had to run and get her and bring her to him. No matter what time of night,

*even if it was two or three o'clock in the morning, this guy had to run and get her. King Solomon lived to be a hundred years old. Do you know how old this guy that was running and getting King Solomon's wives was when he died? He was 30 years old.*

*Don't you know what that proves? That just proves that it's not the women that kill you. It's that running after them that does it![2]*

Of course, Stengel was a hard drinker himself, and sometimes he sent out mixed messages to his players. Mantle liked to tell the story of the time that Stengel, irritated by the team's casual attitude during a losing streak, came up to Ford, Martin, and Mantle in the locker room and said, darkly: "Some of you guys are getting 'whiskey slick.'" He then turned to the rest of the team and added: "I'll tell you another thing. Some of you milkshake drinkers better snap out of it, too!" Unfortunately, none of the three took Stengel's warning to heart. Ford was so amused by Casey's countrified expression that he adopted "Slick" as his nickname.

After decades of barfights, lawsuits, lost jobs, and lost friends, Martin died drunk on Christmas night, 1989, when the pickup truck he was riding in turned over into a ditch. Even though it had little apparent effect on their career statistics, Ford and Mantle continued to abuse alcohol for the rest of their playing days. Mantle's drinking cost him countless friends and any chance at a normal family life. Shortly before he died of liver cancer in 1996, Mantle publicly admitted his lifelong alcoholism and sought professional help. After giving up drinking, Mantle gave several poignant interviews in which he told of his intense unhappiness and begged young baseball fans not to consider him a hero or a role model.

Stengel was not the only member of the Yankee hierarchy to worry about the team's drinking. Weiss, Topping, and Webb all feared for the club's public image; after all, this was the conservative 1950s. As the least indispensable player of the trio, Martin became a useful scapegoat when the Yankees' partying got out of hand. A famous example is the Copacabana nightclub incident, in which a large group of Yankees players including Martin, Mantle, and Ford got into a public fistfight with members of a bowling team. The brawl made headlines, and within days Weiss had publicly blamed everything on Martin. In accordance with Weiss's longstanding policy never to trade a good player to a contending AL club, Stengel's favorite found himself banished to the second-division Kansas City Athletics.

Drinking was not the only reason that Mantle never became the "next Babe Ruth, Lou Gehrig, and Joe DiMaggio rolled up into one" that Stengel dreamed of and that led the Yankees to give Mickey Mantle the number 6 and later the number 7. (Ruth had worn number 3, Gehrig number 4, and DiMaggio 5.) There was also a series of knee and leg injuries that plagued him throughout his career. It all started during the 1951 World Series, in the fifth inning of game two, when Willie Mays—like Mantle, also a rookie—hit a weak fly ball into right center field. Center fielder DiMaggio and right fielder Mantle converged on the ball, but Mantle, giving way to the veteran, pulled up at the last second. As he did so, Mantle caught his spike in a drain cover and crumpled to the ground. He was carried off the field on a stretcher and ultimately underwent surgery to reconstruct his knee. Mantle never regained all of his former speed. Before the injury, Mantle's footspeed had inspired sheer awe. "My God!" Casey Stengel exclaimed the first time he saw Mantle in a sprint, "the boy runs faster than Ty Cobb." Eddie Lopat recalled:

*He was an outstanding center fielder because he could take off and run. He didn't study the batters like DiMag. DiMag was a more astute student of the game than Mickey was. If Mantle would have had DiMag's attitude and his makeup he'd have been the best player of all time, hands down. He was a much better athlete than DiMag. He could run faster than DiMag, and Joe could run!*

Even after he recovered, the Mick had good speed, but the 1951 injury led to others, and those led to more surgery, until by the late 1950s Mantle virtually stopped hitting triples or stealing bases. Worst of all, for most of his 18-year career, Mantle played in terrific pain. "I used to drive Mickey to the ball park," remembered catcher Charlie Silvera, "and after the game I dropped him at his home and Mickey was only 22, 23 at the time and we got to his house and he said, 'I'll see you tomorrow, Charlie.' And he had to lift his legs out of the car with his hands one by one to get out." While some have questioned whether Mickey worked as hard as he could have to rehabilitate his injured legs, no one has ever questioned his courage or willingness to play hard despite great physical pain. In Jim Bouton's classic memoir, *Ball Four*, Mantle's teammates tease the veteran superstar by acting out a scene in the locker room in which a player impersonating manager Ralph Houk begs Mantle to play in spite of the fact that his leg is completely severed at the knee; the Mantle character offers to put the pieces together with scotch tape and try to play.

Two things Mantle could always do were get on base—he was walked once or twice a game by terrified pitchers for most of his career—and hit home runs. He hit them from both sides of the plate; he hit them far and hit them often. As the 1950s wore on, Yankee fans expected that someday soon the big-swinging, muscular Mantle would mount a challenge to Babe Ruth's ancient record of 60 home runs in a season. But in 1956, Mickey Mantle began to change his approach. Asked about his chances of hitting 60 homers, he said that he would rather win the Triple Crown (leading the league in batting average, homers, and RBIs). Mickey then proceeded to go out and do it. In the

*Mickey Mantle carries his bats in this 1953 photo. The switch-hitter was one of the greatest hitters in major-league history, joining Ruth, Gehrig, and DiMaggio as a Yankees immortal.*

season opener at Washington, Mantle became the first batter ever to hit two home runs over the distant, center field fence. "Both those drives had to be over 500 feet," commented Yankees coach Bill Dickey. "The only ball I ever saw clear that fence before was hit by Ruth. But Mantle did it twice in one game."

With 47 home runs entering September, Mantle excited speculation that he might win the Triple Crown and beat Ruth's home-run record at the same time, but suddenly he seemed to lose his long-ball stroke, and he hit only five more the rest of the way. Going into the final series of the season, a three-game affair in Boston, Mantle was comfortably ahead in home runs and RBIs—he would finish with 52 homers, 20 more than Indians slugger Vic Wertz, and 130 RBIs, a few better than Detroit's Al Kaline—but he was tied with Ted Williams in batting average at .348. Mantle bunted safely twice in the series and finished eight points ahead of Williams at .353. "If I could run like him," a disappointed Williams commented, "I'd hit .400 every year!" Mantle's achievement is magnified by the fact that he was only the fourth player ever to lead the majors, not just one league, in all three Triple Crown categories. Nineteen fifty-six turned out to be the only season Mantle ever led the league in batting or RBIs, although he did later bat higher than .353 (.365 in 1957) and he did hit more homers (54 in 1961), and it was a magical year for Mantle, one in which, as he said, "I was healthy most of the season and everything just kind of fell into place."

In 1991, Mantle published a memoir of that year, titled *My Favorite Summer*. In the book he tells the story of how he led the Yankees to the AL flag over Cleveland by nine games and to the world championship over the Brooklyn Dodgers in seven games. In the off-season, after Mantle was voted the first of his three career MVP awards, George Weiss gave him a raise from $32,500 to $65,000. In 1957 the club won the AL pennant again. Mantle hit .365, but with only 34 home runs and 94 RBIs. Weiss rewarded him with a contract offer of $55,000. Mantle could not believe it; he was, in effect, being cut $10,000 for not winning the Triple Crown. Remember that these were the days of the reserve clause; each major league contract contained a provision that allowed ownership to renew the contract, even at a lower salary, indefinitely and without the consent of the player. That meant that players were almost completely under the thumb of management. If they did not accept the contract terms they were offered, they could go out and get another job—outside of organized baseball. No professional club would sign them while they were reserved by another club. Owners Topping and Webb intervened and eventually gave Mantle a contract for $75,000, but his bitterness over the affair never entirely went away.

By the early 1960s, Mickey Mantle finally began to achieve the status of previous Yankee heroes like Ruth, Gehrig, and DiMaggio. As Ruth and Gehrig became ancient history for most fans, America came to revere the apparently humble, small-town kid who gave it his all on every swing and whose teams won so often and—it seemed—so effortlessly. The supporting cast changed through the years. Rizzuto, Coleman, McDougald, Martin, and even Casey Stengel eventually moved on. But Mantle and the Yankees playing in the World Series seemed to be as much a part of the natural order of things as the leaves turning colors in the fall.

Mickey Mantle was an idol to the same American generations that loved Frank Sinatra, James Dean, and Elvis Presley. Everyone from softball players to Little Leaguers wanted to wear Mantle's number 7 on their backs; millions of little boys imitated Mantle's head-down, slightly gimpy home run trot. By the time Mickey Mantle retired in 1968, he put together one of the winningest records of any player in history. He had 536 home runs, a 6.6 percent career home run percentage, and 1,734 bases on balls. He remains in the top ten all-time in all of these categories today. He batted .298 for his career, with 2,415 hits. Perhaps the most impressive of Mantle's numbers is this: in 18 big-league seasons, he played on 12 pennant-winning teams and seven world champions. Today, he holds the records for most World Series homers, 18, most runs scored in the World Series, 42, most RBIs, 40, and most bases on balls, 43. As teammate Tom Tresh said,

*I played with Mickey the last seven years of his career until he retired. He was a really fine person. He had pressures that you and I will never know but he handled them pretty darn well. He was born to be a great hero. I believe that. Certain players have this magnetism—you can't train it. He was just this kid who came out of Oklahoma with blond hair and looked like what America was supposed to be.*[3]

# CHAPTER
# THREE

# 𝒮udden Death: The Best Pennant Race of the 1950s

On October 3, 1951, New York City was ready to make baseball history. The Brooklyn Dodgers and New York Giants were preparing to meet that day in the third and rubber game of a three-game playoff for the National League pennant. Even before the first pitch was thrown, there was a feeling in the air that something wonderful was about to take place. There were 34,320 fans in the stands of the Polo Grounds, the Giants' Manhattan home ballpark, but a crowd, literally, of millions of fans from all around the globe tuned into the game on the NBC, Liberty Mutual, and Armed Services radio networks. Fans lucky enough to own televisions could watch the action at home; the 1951 playoff series was the first sporting event ever to be televised live from coast to coast. The announcing team of Ernie Harwell and Russ Hodges took turns moving back and forth from TV to radio. As if to underline the proud past of the New York Giants and the team's ancient blood feud with archrival Brooklyn, Blanche McGraw, the widow of legendary Giants manager John McGraw, was in attendance.

Brooklyn and New York had formally united under the

name New York City shortly before the turn of the century. Ironically, it was about this time that the baseball fortunes of the New York and Brooklyn baseball clubs began to diverge radically. Under former Baltimore Orioles manager Ned Hanlon, Brooklyn won NL pennants in 1899 and 1900. After that, the club fell into a rut that saw it finish in the second division 28 out of the next 38 seasons. Meanwhile, John McGraw's New York Giants won ten NL pennants and finished second eleven times. This did not mean the end of the New York–Brooklyn rivalry. Far from it: Brooklyn's loyal fans still had as many as twenty-two chances each season to boo and heckle the hated orange-and-black of the Giants. The same went for New York fans and the Dodger royal blue. As one Brooklyn fan remembered, "I always hated the Giants, because they were so classy. The Giants would come in, with Bill Terry, Travis Jackson, Mel Ott, JoJo Moore, and strut onto the diamond like, 'What score shall we win by today?'"

On the rare occasions when Brooklyn was heard from in the NL pennant race, it always seemed to be at the expense of the Giants. In 1914, after the bitter end of his long friendship with McGraw, Giants coach Wilbert "Uncle Robby" Robinson took over as Brooklyn manager. Robinson won the 1916 pennant with a club that included ex-Giants such as catcher John "Chief" Meyers and starting pitcher Richard "Rube" Marquard. John McGraw could not stand losing to Robinson; in the middle of the season finale between the Giants and Dodgers, an irate McGraw caused a minor scandal when he walked off the field in a huff, mumbling that his players were "quitters" who were intentionally throwing the game. In 1920 Uncle Robby and the Dodgers won again, this time in a close race against McGraw's Giants; New York returned the favor by edging out Brooklyn for the 1924 flag.

From 1925 through 1938 Brooklyn lost with numbing regularity, finishing in sixth place eight times under a burned-out Robinson and his equally unsuccessful successor, Casey Stengel. Brooklyn fans did find something positive to get excited about in 1934, when an awful Brooklyn club came to life and knocked New York out of the pennant hunt on the final weekend of the season. The team drew its inspiration from Giants manager Bill Terry's infamous question in a preseason interview: "Is Brooklyn still in the league?"

When the 1940s and 1950s saw both the Giants and Dodgers rebuild into perennial pennant contenders, fans were treated to the glory days of the New York-Brooklyn rivalry. Adding spice to the teams' on-field battles were the class differences between Manhattan and Brooklyn that had developed since the turn of the century. As the home of the unwashed working class and the sons and daughters of poor immigrants, Brooklyn was considered a grimy, slightly disreputable place whose residents spoke the comic dialect known as "Brooklynese." Entertainers of the 1940s and 1950s could get an automatic laugh from any audience west of the Hudson River merely by mentioning the word Brooklyn. The island of Manhattan, on the other hand, monopolized the glamour, wealth, and style of the world's greatest and most sophisticated metropolis. Giants fans ridiculed Brooklyn and its fans as losers; Dodger fans hated New Yorkers for being winners, in baseball and in everything else. To New York fans of that time, there was a lot more riding on those twenty-two games a year between the Dodgers and Giants than who won and who lost. For many, the Dodgers versus the Giants was not a sporting event, it was a matter of self-respect.

Another thing that made the New York–Brooklyn rivalry unique was the fact that, unlike gentler rivalries such as that between the AL Yankees and the Boston Red Sox, the players felt it as intensely as the fans. In 1951, the bitter brew of a Dodgers-Giants pennant race was made toxic by the personalities involved. In 1948 Leo Durocher, the Dodgers' swaggering, skirt-chasing, sharp-dressing manager, had fallen out with team president Branch Rickey and—

to the shock of millions—was immediately hired to manage the Giants. Burt Shotton took over as manager of the Dodgers; he was succeeded in 1951 by former Durocher sidekick Charley Dressen. There was little love lost between the two former colleagues. As Brooklyn pitcher Clem Labine said:

> Charley always wanted to beat Leo, because he used to be his coach, and he always felt that he was much smarter than Leo any day of the week. Charley was willing to tell that to anybody. We had a lot of people who never forgave Leo [for moving to the Giants]. Carl Furillo never forgave Leo, for one.[1]

In his years with Brooklyn, the fiery Durocher had molded the club in his own image. Going against the grain of the laid-back, wait-for-the-home-run philosophy of the times, the Dodgers practiced the fundamentals of Durocher-ball—"sharp spikes, beanballs, and umpire-baiting." Led by Jackie Robinson, Eddie Stanky, and Carl Furillo, they played an aggressive running game, including taking out opposing fielders and runners with menacing hard slides and body blocks that stirred memories of the dead-ball era. They were masters of verbal intimidation. As for the New York Giants, now the shoe was on the other foot; for the first time since the heyday of Ned Hanlon, the Dodgers had the cockiness and swagger of winners. After 1948, with Robinson terrorizing the Giants on the bases and Durocher managing his club from the third-base coaching box, things got very ugly. Durocher hurled unprintable insults at his former protégé, and Robinson responded with crude taunts about Laraine Day, Durocher's glamorous actress wife. When it came to the Dodgers, Giants ace Sal Maglie, called "The Barber" because he liked to "shave" opposing batters with brushback pitches, violated unwritten major-league law by throwing his high fastball behind

51

hitters' heads instead of up-and-in, where, despite appearances, it is far less likely to inflict serious injury. After being decked by Maglie in a 1955 game, Jackie Robinson took care of business Durocher-style. He decided to drag a bunt down the first baseline so that Maglie would have to cover first base, and then time his run so that the two would arrive at the same instant. Robinson executed the play perfectly; arriving at first, the muscular former college football All-American put his head down and laid a devastating hit on the Giants player. Robinson then looked up and discovered that Maglie had read the play and wisely decided to stay on the mound; the man he had hit and, as it turned out, caused a career-ending injury, was young second baseman Davey Williams. The Giants got their revenge a few innings later, when shortstop Alvin Dark hit a double, but kept on running to third base, where he spiked Robinson badly and provoked a bench-clearing brawl.

Durocher's Giants finished fifth to the Dodgers' third in 1948 and fifth again in 1949, when Brooklyn went 97–57 to win the NL pennant. In 1950, New York improved to third, but the Dodgers finished a close second to the "Whiz Kid" Phillies. Far more talented than the Giants, the Dodgers were entering the prime of one of the all-time great NL dynasties, but Leo Durocher was busily rebuilding his club using the same formula that had worked so well in Brooklyn. The 1947 Giants had been the exact opposite of Leo Durocher's idea of a good baseball team. They featured poor pitching, poor defense, and an offense that might be described as slow, stupid, and powerful. Thanks to brawny, one-dimensional uppercutters like Johnny Mize, Willard Marshall, and Walker Cooper, the team set a major-league record by hitting 221 home runs—and came in fourth.

In 1949 Durocher got the smooth, smart double-play combo he wanted when he sent Marshall, Sid Gordon, Buddy Kerr, and Sam "Red" Webb to the Boston Braves for Alvin Dark and second baseman Eddie Stanky, two players he described as "scratchers and divers who are always in the right place at the right time." He shored up the pitching staff—which had only one reliable starter, Larry Jansen—by picking up Sal Maglie after his suspension for jumping to the Mexican League was lifted, and trading for Jim Hearn. He dumped Cooper and replaced him with Wes Westrum, a defensive catcher.

One of the few Giants regulars that Durocher kept was Staten Island–native Bobby Thomson; Thomson was a home-run hitter, but he was young, fast, and a good all-around athlete. Durocher felt the club was ready to compete in 1951—"If we don't win this thing," he told reporters in spring training, "then I don't belong in baseball"—but it started slowly. As Brooklyn pulled ahead early in the pennant chase the Giants put together an 11-game losing streak. Durocher acted decisively and reorganized the team on the fly. He called up rookie outfielder Willie Mays to play center field; moved slugger Bobby Thomson to third base; and put outfielder Whitey Lockman on first.

As the summer of 1951 wore on, the Brooklyn Dodgers rolled over the opposition like a well-oiled tank. Brooklyn had a virtual all-All-Star line up. Behind the plate was Roy Campanella, the NL's answer to Yogi Berra, who would go on to hit 33 home runs with 108 RBIs in 1951. At first was Gil Hodges and his 40 homers and 103 RBIs. At third was the acrobatic glove man Billy Cox. Right and center fields were patrolled by rifle-armed Carl Furillo and Edwin "Duke" Snider, who hit 45 home runs and drove in 192 runs between them. The heart of the team was the Hall of Fame double-play combination of Harold "Pee Wee" Reese and perennial MVP candidate Jackie Robinson, who together scored 200 runs, stole 45 bases, and hit 29 homers. The Dodgers starting pitching was handled by the trio of hard-throwing Don Newcombe, curveballing Carl Erskine, and spitball and junk specialist Preacher Roe. The second line consisted of righty curveball pitcher Clem Labine and a tall 25 year-old pitcher named Ralph Branca, who had caused a stir by going 21–12 in 1947, his first year in a major-league pitching rotation. Branca, who had reverted to a spot starting role in recent years, flouted superstition by wearing the uniform number 13.

By July, young Willie Mays and Bobby Thomson were hitting, Sal Maglie and Larry Jansen were winning, but the increasingly frustrated Giants could not gain any ground on Brooklyn. The Dodgers seemed to be cruising full-speed toward another World Series when they finished July with a 10-game winning streak. Even worse, they were dominating the head-to-head matchups; Brooklyn had taken nine of their first twelve meetings with the Giants going into a critical August series between the two clubs at Brooklyn's Ebbets Field. The Dodgers swept all three games. As the dejected Giants undressed after the game, they heard a loud, banging noise. On the other side of the door that separated the home team and visitors' clubhouses, Jackie Robinson was leading a chorus of Dodgers in an impromptu victory song: "Roll out the barrel," they sang, beating a polka beat on the floor with their bats, "we got the Giants on the run!" Giants infielder Bill Rigney described the reaction of his teammates: "We all knew they had buried us by sweeping the series. Because they had kicked our butts, we had to sit there and take it. But we didn't forget. We knew who was singing. We heard Branca and Jackie, and Jackie was pounding on the door with a bat." A few days later, Durocher's club lost to Philadelphia to put the team 13½ games behind Brooklyn with 44 games remaining.

What followed is one of the greatest turn-arounds in baseball history. There was no Dodgers collapse; the Giants closed the gap all by themselves, going an amazing 37–7, including a 16-game winning streak, the rest of the way. With the two clubs tied on the final morning of the season, New York beat Boston, 3-2, in a nailbiter, in its final regular-season game. A loss by the Dodgers would make Durocher's Giants NL champions. Meanwhile in

Philadelphia, the 22–3 Preacher Roe was unaccountably rocked by the Phillies; the valiant Dodgers hit their way back to send the game into extra innings. With the score tied 8-8 in the top of the fourteenth, Jackie Robinson drove a 1-1 pitch out of the park for a home run; the Dodgers and Giants finished the season in a tie.

By NL rules, the two teams would play a three-game series to decide the pennant. Naturally, the teams split the first two games of the series. The 1951 NL pennant came down to one game, on October 3, at the Polo Grounds between the two staff aces, Don Newcombe for Brooklyn and Sal Maglie for New York. It was an even pitching matchup. Newcombe had posted a 20–9 record during the season, going 5–2 versus the Giants. The 23–6 Maglie had won five out of six from the Dodgers. The winners would meet the New York Yankees the following day in the World Series.

The pennant game began like any other Dodgers-Giants meeting. Brooklyn lead-off batter Carl Furillo dug in at the plate. Pitcher Maglie, with a dark 5 o'clock shadow accentuating his trademark scowl, toed the rubber and looked in for Westrum's sign. "Come on, Sal," Durocher shrieked from the dugout, "Stick it in his ear!" Maglie struck out Furillo, but then issued back-to-back walks to Pee Wee Reese and Duke Snider. Durocher could see that Maglie, who was closing in on 300 innings for the season, was leaving his pitches up in the strike zone, a classic symptom of tiredness. Since there was no tomorrow, he told starter Larry Jansen to start warming up. Jackie Robinson, who had come through in the clutch for the Dodgers all season long, singled sharply to drive in Reese, and Dodgers fans everywhere rejoiced. But Maglie settled down and retired left-fielder Andy Pafko and Gil Hodges to get out of the inning.

Big Don Newcombe blew one powerful fastball after another past the Giants' hitters in the bottom of the inning. In the top of the second the cagey Maglie adjusted for his

lack of stuff by taking more off his curveball and exagger-
ating his customary pattern of alternating pitches up and in
and low and away; the tactic worked and the Brooklyn hitters looked confused and off-balance. Whitey Lockman
singled in the Giants' half of the inning and advanced to
second when Bobby Thomson smacked a line drive into
the left-field corner. The joy of the home crowd turned
quickly to apprehension, however, when Thomson, running with his head down and wrongly assuming that Lockman would try for third, ran into an easy out at second
base. The Giants failed to score.

It was still 1-0 in the home fifth when Thomson doubled with one out. He, at least, was having no trouble
catching up with the Newcombe heater. But Mays struck
out, allowing Newcombe to pitch around Westrum and
escape the inning by striking out pitcher Maglie. Still
searching in vain for his big, sharp-breaking curveball,
Maglie continued to get the Dodgers out with smoke and
mirrors. Then, in the bottom of the seventh, Newcombe
finally weakened. Outfielder Monte Irvin, 32 years old but
because of the baseball color line playing in his first full
major-league season, doubled to left. Durocher played it
by the book, which meant going for the tie at home and
going for the win on the road. In his attempt to sacrifice
Irvin, the tying run, over to third base, Lockman beat out
the bunt to put men on first and third with none out.
Thomson, the next hitter, was thinking sacrifice fly. Now
riding a streak of 21 consecutive scoreless innings, Don
Newcombe was thinking strikeout. He pumped five
straight fastballs across the plate for strikes; Thomson
fouled off the first four but then got around enough to lift a
fly ball to medium center field. Conceding the run, a non-
chalant Duke Snider gloved the ball and tossed it softly
into the infield. It was as if he knew what was about to
happen.

All game long, Maglie had been walking a tightrope
against the explosive Brooklyn lineup. In the top of the

56

eighth, he slipped. Reese singled with one out. Then Snider singled him to third. A nervous Maglie uncorked a 55-foot curve ball that skidded past Westrum and allowed Reese to score the go-ahead run. Durocher then ordered Robinson walked intentionally. The tactic almost worked, as Pafko topped a grounder down the third baseline. Bobby Thomson later said that he felt a strange "positive feeling" throughout the game, but to the Giants fans in the Polo Grounds that day it looked more like Thomson was running for goat of the year, unopposed. He booted Pafko's potential force-out; as the ball rolled into foul territory, Snider scored and the swift Robinson sprinted all the way to third. Finally, a two-out hard liner off the bat off Billy Cox appeared to go right through Thomson, and Robinson scored to make it 4-1 Brooklyn. When the Giants went down one, two, three in the bottom of the eighth, many in the stands began to pack up and head home.

As Larry Jansen took over for Maglie in the ninth, there was a single ray of hope for New York. The Dodgers bullpen was busy; Carl Erskine and Ralph Branca were warming up quickly. Perhaps Newcombe was finally running out of steam. Quietly, Jansen retired the Dodgers in order. The New York Giants had one more chance. To win the NL pennant, the New York Giants needed to score three runs before they made three outs.

Newcombe got ahead of Alvin Dark 0-2 to start the bottom of the ninth, but Dark slapped the third pitch off Hodges's glove into right field for a single. Next up was Don Mueller. Noticing that, for some reason, Dressen had Hodges holding Dark—whose run was, of course, meaningless—close to first base, Mueller aimed another single through the right side. Dark scampered to third. Suddenly, with NL RBI leader Monte Irvin at the plate, representing the tying run, things did not look so bleak for New York. The ballpark buzzed as thousands of fans turned around and made their way back to their seats. Manager Dressen later said that he almost brought in Branca right there, but changed his mind; Newcombe then got Irvin to pop harmlessly to Hodges for the first out. The big Dodgers right-hander pitched carefully to the left-handed Lockman, not wanting to give him a pitch to pull into the right-field seats, but Lockman was going with the pitch all the way. He drove a Newcombe fastball over third base and down the left-field line. Dark scored to make it 4-2; when the dust settled Mueller and Lockman, the tying runs, were in scoring position at second and third.

The Giants players cheered and whooped and slapped each other on the back; the Polo Grounds crowd sent up a deafening roar. What came next was a melodramatic touch that no movie audience would buy, even in a fictional story. The cheering died down and all eyes turned to third base, where Don Mueller was on the ground, writhing in pain. He had badly sprained his ankle sliding into the base and had to be carried off the field on a stretcher. During the lengthy delay, the normally decisive Charlie Dressen held a team meeting on the mound. "Fellas," he said to Reese, Robinson, and Hodges, "what do you think? It's your money as much as it's mine. What do you want to do with it?" This rattled many of the Brooklyn players; they had never seen Dressen seem so nervous, and they had certainly never been asked for their advice on a managing decision. When, Reese gave his opinion that Newcombe had nothing left, Dressen took the ball and called for Branca.

In Bill James's 1988 classic, *The Bill James Historical Abstract*, there appears a sidebar note on the 1951 Giants-Dodgers playoff game under the heading "1951: Where is Earl Weaver when you need him?" James is referring to the advances that Weaver and later managers have made in the area of collecting and interpreting statistics, particularly hitter versus pitcher matchups. Today, thanks in part to computers, every major league manager knows which of his hitters has gone 8-9 against a particular pitcher and which has gone 0-15. This kind of information is often the reason behind mysterious lineup changes or pinch-hitting decisions that leave fans scratching their heads. Back in the 1950s, however, with the possible exception of Casey Stengel, no manager kept track of such things. If they had, Ralph Branca would never have pitched on October 3, 1951. If they had, Charlie Dressen would have known that the Giants had hit ten home runs off Branca that season and had beaten him an incredible five times. Bobby Thomson hit two of those home runs.

As Thomson came to the plate, in the on-deck circle rookie Willie Mays was fighting an attack of nerves. Mays was convinced that Dressen would walk the bases loaded in order to face him, but Dressen never even considered putting the possible winning run on base. Thomson later recalled that he had no sensation of nervousness or any consciousness of the crowd or the weight of the situation. The only thought in his mind was the simple pitching pattern that Branca usually employed against him: using the fastball in on the hands to set up the breaking pitch away. "Strike one!" the umpire called as Thomson took Branca's first pitch down the middle. Feeling a surge of confidence, Branca put fastball number two right where Thomson was looking for it. The Giants hitter opened up, pulled in his hands, and caught the baseball square on the sweet spot of the bat. Everyone in the ballpark jumped up and followed the path of the ball as it flew over Pafko, carried over the Polo Grounds high left-field wall, and landed in the seats. Up in the radio booth, Giants broadcaster Russ Hodges was screaming himself hoarse. This how it sounded to millions of radio listeners.

> Thomson hits a long drive. It's going to be, I believe, the Giants win the pennant! The Giants win the pennant! The Giants win the pennant! Bobby Thomson hit one into the lower deck of the left field stands. The Giants win the pennant! They're going crazy! Oh boy!

*This photograph captures Bobby Thomson's pennant-winning home run against the Brooklyn Dodgers on October 3, 1951. The dotted line shows the ball's trajectory into the stands.*

Down on the field, Thomson jumped and skipped for joy as the Giants and their fans poured out onto the field to celebrate. Ralph Branca walked off the mound with his head down, the number 13 on his jersey looking unnaturally large. The rest of the defeated Dodgers fielders—except one—were shuffling, as if in shock, toward the

*Teammates mob Bobby Thomson, whose dramatic
ninth-inning home run at the Polo Grounds propelled
the Giants into the 1951 World Series.*

visitors' dugout. Jackie Robinson, the consummate com-
petitor, was purposefully circling the bases, following
Bobby Thomson and making sure that he touched every
one.

# CHAPTER FOUR

# "Who's a Bum?": The Dodgers' NL Dynasty

After decades of playing such comically inept baseball that they became known as "Dem Bums"—the unofficial team symbol was a hobo caricature drawn by *Daily News* cartoonist Willard Mullin—the Brooklyn Dodgers startled baseball fans everywhere by achieving respectability in the late 1930s. The team even began to win pennants in the early 1940s. Much of the credit for the Dodgers' resurrection has been given to Branch Rickey, although the team began to turn around earlier, with the arrival of Rickey protégé Larry MacPhail in Brooklyn in 1938. MacPhail acquired shortstop and manager Leo Durocher from Branch Rickey's Cardinals; he also hired broadcaster Red Barber and made the Dodgers the first New York City club to air all of its regular-season games on the radio. Not only did Barber become a beloved figure in New York City, but elsewhere as well. The combination of Barber's personal charm, his soft Mississippi drawl, and Brooklyn's extensive radio network won the team millions of fans across the nation, but especially down South. MacPhail brought in talented players such as first baseman Dolf Camilli, second baseman Billy Herman, shortstop Pee Wee Reese, pitchers

Whitlow Wyatt and Hugh Casey, and outfielder Dixie Walker. The line-drive hitting RBI-man Walker became so popular that he was given the Brooklynese nickname "The Peeple's Cherce."

The team rose from seventh in 1938 to third in 1939 to second in 1940. Branch Rickey then pitched in with a series of trades made while he was serving as St. Louis Cardinals general manager. The revitalized Dodgers were now one of the NL's more profitable franchises, and Rickey sold or traded the following players from the overflowing St. Louis farm system to the free-spending MacPhail: slugging outfielder Joe Medwick, catchers Mickey Owen and Herman Franks, pitcher Curt Davis. When outfielder Pete Reiser, Rickey's prize prospect, was released from a St. Louis minor-league contract by Commissioner Landis in one of his periodic attacks on Rickey's organization, Reiser also moved over to the Dodgers and blossomed, hitting .343 with 39 doubles, 17 triples, and 117 runs scored in 1941, his first full season in the majors. That season saw the Dodgers win their first NL pennant since the regime of Wilbert "Uncle Robby" Robinson in 1920. MacPhail's club also smashed its all-time attendance record, drawing an amazing 1,220,000 of the 4,777,647 fans who passed through all NL turnstiles that year.

In spite of all this success, Durocher and MacPhail were a terrible personal mismatch. The hyperaggressive compulsive gambler Durocher and the unpredictable, compulsive drinker MacPhail had a doomed, love-hate relationship that made Billy Martin and George Steinbrenner look like a pair of love birds. Both had immense egos to go along with their immense baseball talent, and both recognized the abilities of the other. But there was a saying about MacPhail that "with no drinks he was brilliant, with one drink he was a genius, with two he was insane; and rarely did he stop at one." Under the influence of alcohol MacPhail would become dictatorial and capricious, and Leo Durocher was the wrong person to try to push around.

MacPhail would call Durocher to curse him out and fire him. The next morning, as Durocher learned after the first of these phone calls, MacPhail would remember nothing of what had been said and Durocher would still have his job. Still, the constant fighting and bickering between the two got worse and worse, until at the end of the 1942 season a burned-out MacPhail was forced out by the conservative bankers that owned the Dodgers. He surprised everyone by returning to the army as a colonel.

The club replaced MacPhail with Branch Rickey, who had more or less finished his work in St. Louis; led by Stan Musial, the Cardinals were currently the dominant team in the NL. Over the next decade and a half, Rickey built on the foundation laid by MacPhail and created baseball's third great baseball dynasty, after the St. Louis Cardinals of the 1930s and 1940s—also, of course, built by Rickey—and the New York Yankees.

The Dodgers of the 1940s were a rowdy, hard-partying lot that reflected both Leo Durocher's Gas House Gang mentality and Larry MacPhail's affection for colorful characters. One of the most colorful was foul-mouthed, womanizing pitcher Kirby Higbe. According to legend, while on his way home from serving in the Pacific in World War II, Higbe sent his wife a telegram that read: "Arriving April 1. Meet me on the dock if you wish to be first." Higbe's closest friend on the team was relief pitcher Hugh Casey, a bad-tempered alcoholic who hung around with an assortment of gamblers, mob guys, and—when the team was training in Cuba—hard-drinking novelist Ernest Hemingway. Medwick, Walker, and Owen were all rough, even crude types, who would have felt quite at home on the Cardinals of the mid-1930s. Another feature of those Dodgers clubs was the large number of southerners on the team roster: Reese, Arky Vaughn, Walker, Lew Riggs, Higbe, Casey, and Whitlow Wyatt all came from south of the Mason-Dixon line.

After the arrival of Branch Rickey, however, the Dodgers began to change. Concerned for the club's image after Durocher was suspended by Commissioner Chandler for socializing with gamblers and after Brooklyn Catholic groups made an issue of Durocher's sordid private life, Rickey finally let his popular and successful manager go to the rival New York Giants in late 1948. One by one, Rickey then rid the team of the rowdy, hard-drinking element; perhaps in anticipation of his signing of African-American Jackie Robinson, Rickey also began to weed out most of the southerners. By 1949, Wyatt, Higbe, Casey, Medwick, Owen, Walker, and Riggs were gone, their places taken by a combination of clean-cut, responsible types such as first

*Branch Rickey (right) succeeded Larry MacPhail (left) as general manager of the Brooklyn Dodgers in 1942. Building on the foundation laid by MacPhail, Rickey turned the Dodgers into a dynasty.*

baseman Gil Hodges, right fielder Carl Furillo, and center fielder Duke Snider, and classy African-American talent—the cream of which Rickey had grabbed for himself when the baseball color line fell in 1947—such as slugging catcher Roy Campanella and starting pitcher Don Newcombe.

These were special players, spiritually tempered by the extraordinary pressure of wrestling—with the whole nation watching—with the weighty moral issues of Rickey's attempt to integrate baseball, while at the same time battling the more ordinary pressures of playing baseball in a pennant race. Once the experiment had succeeded, the emotional center of the team became infielder Jackie Robinson, the man Rickey had chosen to be first across the color line. Robinson turned out not only to have the heart and courage to be what Rickey would have called a "credit to his race," but to have enough of both qualities left over to become the acknowledged team leader, regardless of race, of one of the greatest teams of baseball players that ever played.

## THE YEAR: 1953

Ted Williams was drafted in 1953 and went to Korea as a Marine Corps fighter pilot, leaving Al Lopez's Cleveland Indians to try to prevent Casey Stengel from winning his fifth consecutive pennant with the Yankees and setting a major-league record. The Indians featured MVP Al Rosen, who missed winning a Triple Crown by a single batting average point. Rosen led the league in RBIs with 145 and homers with 43 but finished second in batting to Senators first baseman Mickey Vernon, .337 to .336. The Yankees, however, simply had too much hitting and too much pitching. Even though no Yankee hit more than Berra's 27 home runs, the club as a whole had seven regulars in double figures in home runs and scored 801 runs overall, the most in the AL. Led by 21-game winner Bob Lemon and 18-game winner Mike Garcia, the Indians pitching was good, but not in the same league as New York's.

Eddie Lopat, Johnny Sain, and Whitey Ford all placed in the top five in ERA—Lopat took the ERA title at 2.42— and the top five Yankee hurlers had records of 18–6, 14–7, 13–6, 16–4, and 13–7. The club allowed the fewest runs in the AL by a wide margin and finished with a record of 99–52. Cleveland was second at 92–62; Led by swift Cuban outfielder Orestes "Minnie" Minoso, Paul Richards's surprising White Sox came in third with a record of 89–65.

The 1953 Dodgers, possibly the greatest Brooklyn club ever, dominated the NL. Hitting on all cylinders, they left an upstart Milwaukee Braves club in their dust after the All-Star break. MVP Roy Campanella hit 41 home runs and led the NL in RBIs with 142. Duke Snider hit 42 out of the park, and Carl Furillo won the NL batting title at .344. Playing left field, his fourth position as a regular with Brooklyn, Jackie Robinson batted .329 and drove in 95 runs. The club as a whole scored an awesome 955 runs, nearly 200 more than the next club, and led the NL in home runs, batting average, stolen bases, fielding average, and pitcher's strikeouts. The Dodgers coasted in 13 games ahead of a strong Braves team that was the talk of baseball. Still, Brooklyn lost a six-game World Series to the Yankees; the Yankees' big weapon was Billy Martin, who had a series that Babe Ruth would have been proud of. "We was beat," Brooklyn manager Charlie Dressen commented, "by a .257 hitter."

After finishing seventh in Boston in 1952, Braves owner Lou Perini had moved the franchise to Milwaukee, Wisconsin, where he found nothing but success. Starving for major-league baseball and thrilled by the Braves' surprising leap over the fading Cardinals into pennant contention, fans turned out in droves. The Braves surpassed their entire 1952 attendance total after a mere thirteen home dates in 1953; for the year they drew nearly two million and set a franchise record. The Braves relied on lefty Warren Spahn, who went 23–7 with a league-leading 2.10 ERA, Lew Burdette, and Johnny Antonelli, who led a staff that combined for a league-low 3.30 ERA; the club's other strength was its slugging lineup of Joe Adcock, Eddie Mathews (the NL home run leader with 47), Andy Pafko, and Sid Gordon.

The Brooklyn Dodgers of the 1950s represented Branch Rickey's highest achievement in baseball, a beautifully balanced set of complimentary parts that hit, ran, threw, fielded, and pitched better than the rest of the NL year in and year out for more than a decade.

*The 1951 Dodgers' lineup featured Duke Snider, Gil Hodges, Jackie Robinson, Pee Wee Reese, and Roy Campanella.*

At first base from 1948 through 1959 was righty Gil Hodges, a big soft-spoken slugger who quietly hit for average and power without ever leading the league in a major hitting statistic. His prime, 1951 through 1956, more or less coincided with that of left-handed teammate Duke Snider, giving Brooklyn three players, along with Campanella, who were a threat to hit 40 homers in a given season. In those years Hodges hit 40 or more twice and scored or drove in 100 or more runs eight times. Light-hitting glove man Billy Cox played a spectacular third base for Brooklyn in the early 1950s; after that the position was shared by several players, including Jackie Robinson, who moved across the diamond to make way for smooth-fielding second baseman James "Junior" Gilliam.

Anchoring the Brooklyn defense was Pee Wee Reese, who played a steady shortstop for the club day in and day out for most of two decades. Standing only 5 feet 10 inches and weighing 160 pounds, the young Reese was a poor hitter, but through hard work and smarts he gradually transformed himself into an effective table setter for the Dodgers' sluggers. A typical season from the middle of Reese's career would be a .280 batting average with 25 doubles, 15 homers, 90 walks, 100 runs scored, and 25 stolen bases. Born on a Kentucky farm, Reese first attracted major-league scouts in 1938 while playing for the Kentucky Colonels, a minor-league club controlled by the Boston Red Sox. Everyone expected the Red Sox to call up Reese for the 1939 season, but 32 year-old player-manager Frank Cronin, who also happened to be the starting shortstop, decided to hold onto the job himself. Reese was sold to the Dodgers for $75,000. This became another in the long litany of historic Red Sox mistakes. Cronin was through as a regular by 1942.

In Brooklyn Reese so impressed another shortstop-manager, Leo Durocher, that he quickly won the starting job. Years later, Durocher liked to tell the story about a time in 1940 when Reese came to him for advice. The 21-

year-old Reese had been a spring training sensation, show-ing incredible fielding range, a powerful arm, and poise beyond his years; it was clear to everyone with eyes that the manager was now the second-best shortstop on the club. As Reese approached him, Durocher said to himself, "Finally the kid was coming over to the old master to ask him about playing shortstop." When Durocher asked him what he wanted to know, however, Reese replied: "Skip, where do you buy your clothes?"

Reese's double-play partner from 1947 through 1952 was Jackie Robinson. To a modern fan, the name Jackie Robinson calls up a variety of images that have little or nothing to do with the winning and losing of baseball games: how Robinson's dark brown skin stood out on baseball diamonds that had been dominated by the colors white and green since the late 19th century; the death threats he received in the mail from racist fans; the vile heckling, knockdown pitches, and spikings that he endured from opposing players; Robinson's humiliation at being excluded from team hotels and forced to eat on a bus while his teammates sat in a whites-only restaurant; and Robinson's famous promise to Branch Rickey that he would accept all of this with Christlike passivity until the "Great Experiment" succeeded.

At least as important, however, for the outcome of the "Great Experiment," was Jackie Robinson's success on the field. When the shocking news first broke that Branch Rickey had added Robinson to the 1947 Brooklyn Dodgers, there were many, including friends and team-mates of the Negro League shortstop, who worried that he would fail and set back the cause. He lacked polish; his arm strength was suspect; and he had a tendency to fly off the handle emotionally, especially when confronted with open racism. As a Californian and a star athlete who had played on integrated teams at an integrated college, Robin-son was outraged and bewildered by the Jim Crow cus-toms and laws of the South. The prevailing attitude among his teammates, remembered Negro League star Buck Leonard, was "We don't see how he can make it." But Robinson rose to the occasion splendidly.

Playing first base, a position that does not require a strong arm, he batted .297, scored 125 runs, and took home the NL Rookie of the Year award. In the years that followed, Robinson got even better. He won a batting title and a pair of stolen base crowns. He was unselfish, moving to second base, third base, and then to the outfield to accommodate talented younger players and improve the team. This was in spite of the lukewarm support he got from his teammates, at least in the early years, and the unimaginable abuse he took from many opposing players and fans.

By the early 1950s, after Branch Rickey had traded away the team's unredeemable bigots and most of the rest of the Dodgers closed ranks behind him, Brooklyn counted on Jackie to score and drive in big runs. Even more, the club began to take on Robinson's character, both as a player and as a person. Inspired by his daring and aggressiveness on the basepaths, the Dodgers played a running game that beautifully complimented their home-run power. In a way the club was ahead of its time, employing the same deadly combination of speed and power that characterized the Negro Leagues and that—thanks to Hank Aaron, Frank Robinson, Willie Mays, and a whole talented generation of young African-American stars—would soon become the trademark of the NL.

After 1948, when Robinson was released from his promise to "turn the other cheek" to avoid the kind of ugly racial incident that Branch Rickey was sure would kill any hope of integration in baseball, he gave full vent to his emotions and punished those who got in his way. Seeming to thrive on controversy and opposition, Robinson led the Dodgers to pennant after NL pennant, while at the same time speaking out about racism inside and outside baseball. He fearlessly took on sacred cows, even ripping Yankees icon Casey Stengel for refusing to sign African-American players. As Roger Kahn writes:

> Robinson could hit and bunt and steal and run. He had intimidating skills, and he burned with a dark fire. He wanted passionately to win. He charged at ball games. He calculated his rivals' weaknesses and measured his own strengths and knew—as only a very few have known—the precise move to make at precisely the moment of maximum effect. His bunts, his steals, and his fake bunts and fake steals humiliated a legion of visiting players. He bore the burden of a pioneer and the weight made him more strong. If one can be certain of anything in baseball, it is that we shall not look upon his like again.[1]

Jackie Robinson had a short career; there were only ten seasons between his rookie debut at the age of 28 and his last season with Brooklyn in 1956. Before the 1957 season, new Dodgers owner Walter O'Malley traded Robinson to the New York Giants, an act considered even more unspeakable by Brooklyn fans than the Durocher deal ten years earlier. Rather than play for the Giants, Robinson quit.

If the 1950s Dodgers had a consistent flaw, it was their inability to find a regular left fielder. Gene Hermanski, Andy Pafko, George Shuba, Sandy Amoros, and Gino Cimoli were a few of the men who played left in Ebbets Field without making anyone forget Pete Reiser. From 1949 through 1958, however, center field and right field were set. The right fielder was the dour Pennsylvanian Carl Furillo, and flamboyant Duke Snider played center.

A moody, intense, but incredibly consistent player, Furillo established himself as a regular in 1949, when he batted .322 with 27 doubles, 10 triples, 18 home runs, 95 runs scored, and 106 RBIs. He gave the Dodgers pretty

*Jackie Robinson steals home in the 1955 World Series, beating out the tag by Yogi Berra. Robinson's aggressive play inspired his Dodgers teammates.*

much that same season for the next nine years, finishing his career with a .299 batting average and 192 lifetime homers. Furillo was a good hitter, but his true claim to fame was defense, specifically his uncanny ability to play the tricky caroms produced by Ebbets Field's eccentric right-field wall, which was curved in one place, straight in another, and covered with materials as different as cement, wire mesh, and banks of scoreboard lights. Furillo was called the "Reading Rifle" for the strong and accurate throwing arm that he used to gun down a dozen or more enemy baserunners each season.

Thanks to his beach-boy good looks and all-out style of play, center fielder Duke Snider became an instant fan favorite, the Dodgers' answer to the Yankees' Mickey Mantle and the Giants' Willie Mays. Even if, in hindsight, Snider never really belonged in that league, he was a terrific fielder and a dangerous left-handed batter who was perfectly suited to take advantage of tiny Ebbets Field. Snider reached his prime in 1953, when he batted .336 with 42 homers, 132 runs scored, and 126 RBIs. For the next four seasons in a row, he never hit fewer than 40 home runs and averaged 112 runs and 115 RBIs per season. Snider was famous for two things: circus catches, like the one that helped beat the Phillies on the last day of the 1951 season, and majestic home runs that carried over the right field wall and bounded across Bedford Avenue. His career statistics, .295 batting average with 407 home runs, were greatly hurt by the club's move to the new ballpark in Los Angeles. Snider's home run production fell from 40 in Brooklyn in 1957 to 15 in Los Angeles in 1958 and never recovered.

The last key component of the Brooklyn Dodgers' offense was African-American catcher Roy Campanella. A deceptively plump child prodigy who had played for Baltimore in the Negro National League when he was only fifteen years old, Campanella learned his craft from Negro League legend Raleigh "Biz" Mackey. Campanella was one of the many Negro League stars who, because of the color line, was deprived of at least half a major-league career. He became the Dodgers' regular catcher in 1949 at 28 and held the job through 1957. He handled pitchers beautifully and made bullet-like throws down to second base that bruised middle infielder's hands. In his ten short years in the NL Campanella hit 242 home runs, drove in more than 100 runs three times, set a major-league record for most home runs by a catcher in one season, won three MVP awards, and helped his team to five World Series. Already slowed down by injuries, Campanella's career came to an abrupt end when he was paralyzed in a January 1958 car accident.

Often overshadowed by the hitters, the Brooklyn pitchers of the 1950s were consistently excellent, if not as deep or as dominating as some of the great Yankee staffs of the 1950s. As their World Series showdowns with the Yankees pointed up, the only thing that Brooklyn lacked, in the words of writer Roger Kahn, was "the kind of pitching that makes victory sure"—although, to be fair, the kind of pitching that assured victory over the Yankees did not exist. The mainstays of those Dodgers staffs were Carl Erskine and Don Newcombe. A smallish right-hander with no more than above-average stuff, Erskine used intelligence and control to win between 54 percent and 77 percent of his pitching decisions between the years 1951 and 1957. Known to the fans as "Oisk," Erskine's peak came with the great 1953 team, when he went 20–9 to lead the NL in winning percentage. The majors' first great African-American pitcher, Don Newcombe was a dominating force from his 17–8 debut in 1949 to his sudden decline in 1957. In between he used his explosive fastball to compile records of 19–11, 20–9, 9–8, 20–5, and 27–7. In his prime and in good health, Newcombe's only flaw was that of the entire Brooklyn team: an incomprehensible tendency to collapse at clutch moments. Newcombe gave up a pennant-losing homer in 1950, failed to close out the third game of the 1951 NL playoff, and went 0–4 with a bloated 8.59 ERA in three trips to the World Series.

It was the Brooklyn Dodgers' misfortune to reach their peak in an era that belonged to the New York Yankees of Mickey Mantle, Yogi Berra, and Whitey Ford, although the team was capable of disastrous losses to other opponents as well. Great Brooklyn teams lost in the most heartbreaking circumstances possible to the Phillies on the final day of the season in 1950, to the Giants on the final day of the season in 1951, to the Yankees in the final game of the World Series in 1952, to the Yankees in six World Series games in 1953, and to the Yankees once again in seven games in the World Series of 1956.

In 1955, however, fate finally seemed to smile on Brooklyn fans, who had not seen their club win a single World Series championship in seven tries since the two-league system began in 1903. Managed by Walter Alston, the Dodgers won their first ten games in 1955. After another early-season winning streak, of eleven games, the team was 8½ games ahead of the rest of the league in mid-May. The team never looked back and clinched the NL flag as early as September 8, an NL record. Brooklyn finished 13½ games up on the Milwaukee Braves and prepared for another rematch with the New York Yankees, against whom the mighty 1953 club had made it 0–4 against Stengel's Yankees in the Series.

The Dodgers dropped the first two games of the 1955 World Series at Yankee Stadium, but then, improbably, swept all three games at Ebbets Field thanks to the pitching of left-handed change-up artist Johnny Podres and right-hander Roger Craig, and timely home runs from Campanella, Hodges, and Snider. When Whitey Ford handled the Dodgers easily in game six, winning 5-1, it all came down to the seventh-game matchup between Podres and Yankees lefty Tommy Byrne. Neither of these men could be mistaken for the ace of their staff, but this was somehow fitting for an important Yankees-Dodgers showdown that was also missing Jackie Robinson and Mickey Mantle—both were sidelined by injury. When Podres won a bizarre victory in which every break went his way—the baseball gods seemed to be trying to make up all at once for all the bad luck that had plagued the club in a decade of Octobers—the Brooklyn Dodgers won the world's championship.

While the Brooklyn players rejoiced at finally getting the monkey of perpetual World Series defeat off their backs, the people of Brooklyn went absolutely crazy. The fans who invented the phrase "Wait 'till next year" put on a party that stretched from one end of the borough to the other, from Canarsie to Greenpoint and East New York to Sunset Park. Car horns honked, pots and pans were banged together, and the lawyers and businessmen of Court Street in downtown Brooklyn held an impromptu ticker-tape parade. The next day the *Daily News* featured a gigantic headline reading "THIS IS NEXT YEAR" and an oversized, grinning Willard Mullin hobo with the caption: "Who's a Bum?" Brooklyn's long-suffering fans partied like next year would never come again and, thanks to Dodgers owner Walter O'Malley, it did not. The 1955 World Series championship was Brooklyn's first—and its last. The club would not win it all again until after O'Malley, claiming that he could not survive without higher attendance and a new ballpark, moved the franchise to Los Angeles before the 1958 season.

The Dodgers dynasty is distinguished by having provided America with a positive example of peaceful integration, for its six NL pennants, and for its penchant for last-minute, disillusioning failure on an almost Greek scale. There is one more thing, however, that made the Dodgers special: the team's relationship with its fans and with the city of Brooklyn. The joy of rooting for the Dodgers began with the team's home ballpark, Ebbets Field, which bred a closeness between fans and players that can be found today only in a few minor-league ballparks. "When you have a box seat in Brooklyn," said announcer Red Barber, "you are practically playing the infield." Thanks to the small dimensions of the Brooklyn park and the way the upper deck hung low over the playing field, there was always a lot of give and take between the field and the stands. Ebbets Field developed and nurtured famous fans who were as much a part of the show as the players. There was Hilda Chester, a middle-aged woman who rang a cowbell to bring her team luck, Cookie Lavagetto's one-man rooting section, and the Dodger Sym-Phony, a motley band of Italian-American fans from Greenpoint who, when a visiting batter struck out, would time a loud bass drum beat for the moment his rear end came in contact with the dugout bench.

The Brooklyn players' closeness with the Brooklyn fans was also a by-product of the times. In those days only a handful of ballplayers made salaries that were much greater than those of the fans in the field boxes, and many were paid no better that the fans in the grandstand. This did not make those players any more virtuous or more conscientious than modern players, but it did make them more accessible. Players took the subway to work and could be approached as they walked to and from the ballpark, and they tended to live in the same middle-class Brooklyn neighborhoods as most of their fans. This created a kind of informality and intimacy that is unthinkable today. In Peter Golenbock's oral history of the Dodgers, *Bums*, Irving Rudd tells the following story that took place at Ebbets Field when he was twelve years old:

> *I was hanging around outside the ballpark, holding my scrapbook under my arm, when Al Lopez came out of the clubhouse. He was a kid catcher, about twenty years old, and he's got a guy with him by the name of Hollis Thurston, Bobo Newsom, Jake Flowers, and Clise [Dudley]. I'm standing there in my knickers and Lopez says to me, "Hey kid, how about going to dinner with us?" I said, "Gee, I have to ask my mother." He said, "Give her a call." Who had a phone in those days? A phone in Brownsville? I told them we didn't have a phone. They asked me where I lived, and told them, "Powell Street in Brownsville," and Lopez said, "We'll drop you off on the way home. You ask your mother." So we got into the car, and I sat on Newsom's lap, and they drove me to Brownsville. I went upstairs, and my mother came down to say hello.*

*"Take care of my son," she says. They say "Sure, Mom, don't worry about it." And they took me to a Spanish restaurant near the St. George Hotel. I had arroz con pollo. After they fed me, they brought me back to the hotel, and we sat around till midnight bullshitting about baseball. And then they brought me home.*[2]

With today's players and fans living in two different worlds, physically as well as economically—it is a rare modern player who does not commute to work from a distant wealthy suburb—and kept apart by a wall of security, Rudd's great-grandson would be lucky to get a hasty autograph from one of his idols.

To this day, Brooklyn fans are understandably sentimental about their team and the good old days before 1958. Dodgers nostalgia is a powerful force, but it is also a complicated mixture of positive and negative feelings, among them happy memories of a winning baseball team, fascination with the saga of Jackie Robinson, anger at Walter O'Malley's betrayal of the Brooklyn fans, and a wider nostalgia for lost youth and a bygone way of life. One Dodger fan, lawyer Ira Levine, recalled how he felt when he heard that his hero, Roy Campanella, had died:

*Life [in 1950s Brooklyn] seemed so simple, so innocent. There were family, friends, school, and the Dodgers, and not necessarily in that order of priority. Brooklyn had a love affair with their team, and their team loved them back. The Dodgers were my heroes and my heroes are dying, and as they leave us my youth becomes a little more distant and my mortality a little more apparent. As they die, a little piece of me dies.*

Anyone—any adult, at least—can see the truth of these words. Everyone gets old and mourns the loss of youth, but sports, rigidly divided into seasons, heighten the sensation of the passing of time and of the natural cycle of birth, youth, and death. It is a particular part of being a sports fan to taste vicariously the bitter, premature career death that comes to all athletes, long before real physical death, when their youth is gone.

There are aspects, however, of Brooklyn Dodgers nostalgia that are not quite so profound or even legitimate. For example, a key element of the Dodgers mythology is the idea that the fans loyally supported the team throughout the 1950s and that there was no justification at all for O'Malley to move the franchise to California. Unfortunately, this is not so. Despite the rosy memories of the generation that grew up during those years, the 1950s were a rotten time for the baseball business in general and for the Brooklyn Dodgers in particular. After rising to dizzying heights in the euphoric years just after World War II, major-league attendance fell steadily for a decade, declining from 21 million in 1948 to 17.5 million in 1950 to 14.4 million in 1953. The Braves, Athletics, and Browns were forced to relocate after recording attendance figures that are difficult to believe today. The Boston Braves, for example, drew 281,000 fans for the entire 1952 season; in 1996 it was not unusual for many teams to draw that many fans in a single week.

After drawing 1.8 million in 1946 and roughly the same number again in 1947, the Dodgers saw their attendance decline every year for the next ten seasons. In 1957 barely a million fans came to Ebbets Field. Of course, all of this was happening in the context of the club contending for or winning the NL pennant nearly every year. Brooklyn owner Walter O'Malley saw his team winning and profits shrinking. He asked the government for help in building a modern ballpark to replace decrepit Ebbets Field, something that most major-league cities would agree to do for their local franchises over the next twenty years. He was refused.

80

Where were all the Dodger fans going? Many were leaving the city, along with much of the rest of America's middle class. The combination of the development of attractive new suburbs, highways that made them easy to get to, and racial fears provoked by the arrival of African-Americans and other minorities in previously white city neighborhoods fed on each other and caused the decimation of large areas of Brooklyn and other cities. This, in turn, has created a kind of false nostalgia that covers up feelings of guilt. It goes like this: Once there was no crime, no litter, no racial problems, and everybody rooted for the Dodgers; when the team left, the heart was torn out of Brooklyn, we were abandoned and betrayed, and the city itself went downhill. Perhaps urban life was kinder and gentler in the 1950s than it is today. And there is no question that many Brooklynites felt real hurt and anger when their team left town. There were many others, however, who left the Dodgers before the Dodgers could leave them.

Brooklyn itself has survived the past forty years without a professional baseball team just fine. As the memory of the Giants-Dodgers rivalry fades, the still-knowledgeable and still-passionate Brooklyn fans divide their loyalties between the Queens-based New York Mets, who wear Dodger blue (mixed with Giants orange) and, believe it or not, the once-hated New York Yankees. Yet something remains of the connection between this city and its former baseball team. Visit a New York bookstore in April and count the books that have been published on the subject of the Brooklyn Dodgers. Find another abandoned major-league city that has an active Hall of Fame devoted to its former team or another sports franchise, living or dead, that has had a book written about it in the same league as Roger Kahn's classic *The Boys of Summer*. Or simply walk through Brooklyn and count the number of royal blue baseball caps with an embroidered white "B" that you see, or try to find a pizzeria or tavern that does not display a framed team photo of the 1955 world champions. What you will discover is that while dozens of baseball clubs have left one city for another, only one of them is still missed.

No one mourns—or even much talks about—the Seattle Pilots, the Philadelphia Athletics, or the Boston Braves; very few remember the Browns or the Giants, who were once as big in New York as the Yankees. But the Brooklyn Dodgers dynasty of the 1950s has transcended baseball history. In some mystical way the team remains part of the identity of a community of 2.5 million people, even if most of them were either not yet alive—or else living in China, Jamaica, or Ecuador—the last time Pee Wee Reese threw a runner out from the hole, Roy Campanella smacked a three-run homer, or Jackie Robinson stole home.

# THE YEAR: 1954

The New York Yankees had their finest season in 1954, winning 103 games and leading the AL in runs, batting, and slugging. As if to prove that anything can happen in baseball, however, Al Lopez's Cleveland Indians won the pennant. The Yankees' stats look like those of a winner: Six regulars reached double figures in homers, and the top five pitchers went 20–6, 16–8, 13–4, 12–4, and 11–5. Catcher Yogi Berra won the MVP. It was just that the Indians got 32 homers out of league-leader Larry Doby, 24 from Al Rosen, and 11 or more from half a dozen other players, including new first baseman Vic Wertz; second baseman Bobby

*This sequence captures the most famous catch in major-league history: Willie Mays's breathtaking over-the-shoulder snag in the 1954 World Series.*

Avila hit .341 and won the batting title; and the Indians' pitching was even deeper than New York's. Lemon and Wynn won 23 games apiece, tying for the league lead; Garcia took the ERA title at 2.64. Art Houtteman and Bob Feller went 15–7 and 13–3. The bullpen of Hal Newhouser, Don Mossi, and Ray Narleski went 16–6 with 27 saves. Cleveland won an incredible 111 games, against only 43 losses. At the other end of the standings, Bill Veeck sold the St. Louis Browns to a group who moved the franchise to Baltimore and changed its name to the Orioles. It didn't help; Baltimore finished seventh, just ahead of an Athletics team that itself would move to Kansas City the following season.

In the NL, Willie Mays returned from two years in the army to lead the New York Giants to another upset victory over Brooklyn. The Dodgers suffered off years from Don Newcombe and catcher Roy Campanella, who batted only .207 with 19 home runs. Mays won the NL batting title at .345, hit 41 homers and 13 triples, and drove in 110 runs; he was voted MVP over Cincinnati slugger and home-run leader Ted Kluszewski. Giants pitcher Johnny Antonelli, acquired from Milwaukee for Bobby Thomson, went 21–7 and won the ERA title at 2.30; teammate Ruben Gomez went 17–9. Super reliever Marv Grissom had ten wins and 19 saves. New York swept the World Series, which featured Mays's famous catch off Vic Wertz and a 3-4 pinch-hitting performance, including two clutch home runs, from Giants backup outfielder James "Dusty" Rhodes.

## CHAPTER FIVE

# "Home Run Carnival": The 1952 World Series

Most of the great World Series moments of the 1950s came in the four subway series between the Yankees and the Dodgers. There was Yankees pitcher Don Larsen's perfect game in 1956. There was the 1953 series, in which Billy Martin hit .500 with two triples, two homers, and eight RBIs, and after which Dodgers manager Charlie Dressen was fired. The greatest of all the subway series, however, was the 1952 battle between Casey Stengel's Yankees and Branch Rickey's Dodgers, a tight, seven-game thriller in which each game could have gone the other way.

Both the 1952 Yankees and the 1952 Dodgers were entering the prime years of their respective dynasties and were evenly matched. New York had won 95 regular-season games and Brooklyn, 96. Berra versus Campanella; Mantle versus Snider; Mize versus Hodges; Cox versus McDougald; Reese and Robinson versus Martin and Rizzuto; pitchers Roe, Erskine, Black, and Loes versus their New York counterparts Reynolds, Raschi, Lopat, and Sain—most of the key matchups were dead even or close to it. As for tactical styles, the Dodgers ran more and Charlie Dressen liked the sacrifice bunt a lot more than Casey Stengel, but both clubs played classic 1950s-era baseball, which boiled down to getting men on base and waiting for the home run.

The series as a whole featured a mere six stolen bases—only one by the Yankees—and 16 home runs, ten by the Yankees. In the words of sportswriter and eyewitness Fred Lieb, "In both Yankee Stadium and Ebbets Field, baseballs sailed into the stands like no. 5 golf iron shots." In spite of Mantle's speed, Robinson's daring, Charlie Dressen's compulsive bunting, and both teams' excellent defense, in the end all seven games were decided by the big bang.

The opening game at Ebbets Field pitted New York ace Allie Reynolds, 20–8 with a 2.97 ERA on the season, against rookie reliever Joe Black. The fifth African-American to pitch in the major leagues in the 20th century, the New Jersey–born Black was a big, tough right-hander with a blazing fastball. He had gone 15–4 in 54 relief appearances during the 1952 season, but Dressen gave him three World Series starts, playing a hunch that Black would give the Yankees hitters trouble. He was right. Black won, 4-2, in a nip-and-tuck game in which, typically, it seemed that neither team could score except via the long ball. Robinson hit a solo homer in the second; third baseman Gil McDougald evened the score with a home run in the third. In the fourth, the Yankees failed to cash in on a first-and-third, one-out situation when Brooklyn's Carl Furillo caught Joe Collins's line drive in right field and fired a perfect strike to the plate. In the Yankees' fifth, McDougald walked with none out and was gunned down by left-fielder Andy Pafko when he tried for third on Martin's single. In the bottom of the sixth, Pee Wee Reese singled and then scored on Duke Snider's two-run home run. Finally, the Yankees scored a meaningless eighth-inning run on Gene Woodling's triple and Hank Bauer's sac fly; this was the only run of the game that did not come in on a homer.

# THE YEAR: 1955

One of Casey Stengel's finest achievements was the 1955 season, which saw the Yankees overcome an off-year from Phil Rizzuto, an injury to Jerry Coleman, the loss of Billy Martin to the military draft, and the partial collapse of his aging pitching staff to go 96–58, beating out Cleveland by three games. Led by MVP Yogi Berra, the New York lineup was full of productive part-timers, from shortstop Billy Hunter to catcher Elston Howard to first baseman Eddie Robinson. The pitching staff featured ace Whitey Ford, who went 18–7, and youngsters Bob Turley, Tommy Byrne, Don Larsen, and Johnny Kucks. New York led the AL in homers, finished second in team runs, and recorded a league-best 3.23 ERA. Twenty-two-year-old fireballer Herb Score went 16–10 with an AL-high 245 strikeouts for runner-up Cleveland. In Detroit, 20-year-old outfielder Al Kaline hit .340 to tie Ty Cobb as the youngest player ever to win a batting title. Mickey Mantle won his first home-run title, and the Tigers' Ray Boone and the Red Sox' Jackie Jensen tied for the league lead in RBIs with 116. Chicago's Billy Pierce beat out Ford for the ERA title, 1.97 to 2.63.

In the NL, the Brooklyn Dodgers had their golden "Boys of Summer" season. MVP Roy Campanella hit 32 homers and batted .318; Snider hit .309 with 42 homers and a league-best 136 RBIs. The Dodgers led their league in team runs scored, runs allowed, doubles, homers, batting average, slugging average, stolen bases, and ERA. Don Newcombe had a career year, going 20–5, and reliever Clem Labine won 13 and saved 11. Richie Ashburn of the fourth-place Phillies won the batting title at .338; New York's Willie Mays launched a league-best 51 home runs; and Pittsburgh's Bob Friend took the ERA honors at 2.83. Newcombe was second at 3.20. In the 1955 World Series, the Dodgers beat the Yankees in seven games to win Brooklyn's first world championship since the days of Ned Hanlon and a single major league in the 19th century.

*The 1955 Cleveland Indians pitching staff surrounds manager Al Lopez (in chair). Despite their 93–61 record, the Indians finished three games behind the Yankees in the AL pennant race.*

Nineteen fifty-five saw the passing of two baseball legends. Late 19th- and early 20th-century pitcher Denton True "Cy" Young died of heart failure at 88. Young won more games in his 22-year career, 511, than anyone in history. Starting in 1956, baseball honored Young by giving an annual trophy with his name on it to the major leagues' best pitcher; starting in 1967, two awards were given, one for each league. Former Pirates star shortstop Honus Wagner also died in 1955; many consider him, after Babe Ruth, the best player in history.

Game two of the 1952 World Series, which matched New York's Vic Raschi and Brooklyn's Carl Erskine, stayed close for five innings. New York led, 2-1, going into the top of the sixth, when Erskine suddenly lost it. Mantle reached on a bunt base hit. Woodling singled to center. Berra walked. With Billy Loes in to pitch, Joe Collins hit into a double play, but Gil Hodges dropped the relay from second. McDougald then singled and Mantle added a three-run homer to put New York ahead for good, 7-1. Hodges would go on to become the goat of the series by going 0-21 with six strikeouts.

The next day the series moved across town to the Bronx, where Brooklyn's veteran Preacher Roe faced control pitcher Eddie Lopat. Roe frustrated the Yankees, who loaded the bases in the fourth but failed to score. After eight complete innings, the score was 3-2 Dodgers; New York's runs had scored on an RBI single from Lopat and a solo home run by Yogi Berra. In the top of the ninth Jackie Robinson and Pee Wee Reese worked a double steal against young reliever Tom Gorman, and both men scored on a Berra passed ball. Pinch-hitting for Gorman, Johnny Mize homered in the bottom of the inning to make the final 5-3 in favor of the Dodgers. The Yankees got another look at Joe Black in game four. Allie Reynolds outpitched Black, allowing no runs and striking out ten; Jackie Robinson went 0-4 with three strikeouts, one of them coming with men on first and third in the top of the first. With the Yankees leading 1-0 in the fifth, men on second and third with one out, and pitcher Joe Black at the plate, Dressen put on the suicide squeeze. Black, however, missed the pitch and the lead runner ran into an easy tag out. Substituting at first base for a slumping Joe Collins, left-handed slugger Mize was the hitting star for New York; he homered, doubled, and drew a walk. The series was now tied at two games apiece.

Game five was a must-win situation for the Yankees; if they lost they would go to Brooklyn needing to sweep the series's final two games in order to win. It was a must-win game for the Dodgers for the same reason; they wanted two chances to knock the Yankees off at home. Both sides played with a sense of urgency. In the top of the second, Brooklyn scored first off Yankees starter Ewell Blackwell when Robinson walked, advanced to third on an infield single and a stolen base, and scored on a single by Andy Pafko. Brooklyn loaded the bases in the inning, but pitcher Carl Erskine killed the rally by failing in yet another attempted squeeze play. In the bottom of the inning Pafko leaped high over the right-field wall to rob Gene Woodling of a two-run homer.

The Dodgers added three more runs in the fifth, when Hodges scored on a sac fly from Reese and Duke Snider whacked a two-run homer to right-center. Down 4-0, the dogged Yankees rallied in the bottom of the inning, scoring two runs on a walk to Bauer and singles by Billy Martin, Irv Noren, and Phil Rizzuto. Johnny Mize then hit a three-run homer to give his team a 5-4 lead. Duke Snider tied the score in the seventh by driving in Billy Cox from second with a two-out single. Meanwhile, Erskine regrouped and retired the next 19 batters he faced after Mize's home run.

In the top of the eleventh, Brooklyn broke through against reliever Johnny Sain. Cox singled off McDougald's glove with one out. Reese sent him over to third with a crisp single. Duke Snider then drove Cox in with a double, after which Robinson was walked intentionally and Furillo hit into a 5-2-3 double play. Bucking for series MVP, Mize hit another ball over the right-field wall in the Yankees' half of the inning, but Furillo, a defensive substitute for Pafko in right, jumped up over the barrier and caught it. With their team now leading in the series, three games to two, and with the next two games at home, Brooklyn fans allowed themselves to hope that this might be their first World Series championship. "I think we've got them now," said a confident Walter O'Malley.

# THE YEAR: 1956

The 1956 season belonged to up-and-coming Yankees superstar Mickey Mantle. The 24-year-old slugger won both the Triple Crown, batting .353 with 52 homers and 130 RBIs—a season worthy of Babe Ruth—and the AL MVP. The rest of the New York attack was only slightly less deadly. Berra hit 30 home runs and drove in 105 runs; Hank Bauer and Moose Skowron combined for 49 more home runs and 174 RBIs; and the team as a whole scored 857 runs, 68 more than runner-up Detroit. With Whitey Ford going 19–6 with a league-best 2.47 ERA and Kucks, Larsen, and Sturdivant filling the shoes of the departed Reynolds, Raschi, and Lopat, Stengel's club finished nine games up on the Indians and defeated Brooklyn in a seven-game series that featured the famous game-six no-hitter by Larsen.

In the NL, the Dodgers barely repeated, surviving a tense, three-team race with the Milwaukee Braves and a powerful Cincinnati Reds team that tied a major-league record by hitting 221 home runs. Dodgers ace Don New-combe turned in his finest season, going 27–7 to win both the MVP and the first Cy Young award, which until 1967 was given to the best pitcher in the major leagues, not to the best in each league (as with the MVP). The Braves Hank Aaron won the batting title at .328; Duke Snider led in home runs with 43; and Cardinals immortal Stan Musial won the RBI title with 109. Milwaukee's Lew Burdette and Warren Spahn topped the NL in ERA at 2.70 and 2.78, respectively.

Vic Raschi beat Brooklyn's Billy Loes in game six of the 1952 World Series in a contest so close that it was decided on a play involving both pitchers: Loes's muff of an easy grounder by Raschi back to the mound. Loes's explanation—"I lost it in the sun"—has gone down as one of baseball history's goofiest excuses, but, oddly enough, it was probably the truth. As any old Dodger could tell you, the October sun had a way of setting through the Ebbets Field girders and blinding infielders with glare. Neither team scored until Snider's solo homer in the sixth. The Yankees got two in the seventh on Berra's solo home run and the infamous Raschi bouncer that caromed off Loes and drove in Gene Woodling. Mantle and Snider each homered in the eighth to make the final score Yankees 3, Dodgers 2. For the Dodgers, it was now a one-game series, but they had the home-field advantage. For the Yankees, it was the first time in their many World Series that they had to play a game seven on the road.

Everybody pitched for both teams in the final game: Lopat, Reynolds, Raschi, and Kuzava for New York and Black, Roe, and Erskine for Brooklyn. In the fourth inning, series hero Johnny Mize drove in Phil Rizzuto with an opposite-field single. The game was probably decided in the bottom of the inning, when the Dodgers loaded the bases with no outs on a Snider single and bunt base hits by Robinson and Campanella. Stengel then brought in Allie Reynolds, who allowed a run on a lineout to left by Gil Hodges, but then struck out Shuba and got Furillo to ground out. The score was tied, 1-1, but Brooklyn had wasted a precious opportunity. Gene Woodling hit a solo homer in the fifth; Reese then singled in Billy Cox, who had doubled, to make it 2-2.

After that, the Yankees began, in their inimitable style, to slowly pull away. Mickey Mantle homered deep to right with the bases empty in the sixth and contributed an RBI single his next time up. Brooklyn's last gasp came in the bottom of the seventh, when Vic Raschi walked Furillo and then loaded the bases with one out on a single by Billy Cox and another walk to Pee Wee Reese. Stengel brought in lefty Bob Kuzava to face the red-hot Duke Snider. It was a classic Stengel move in that it was surprising—the young left-hander was making his first and only appearance in the series—it gave the Yankees the platoon advantage, and it worked. A reliever and spot-starter who had appeared in only 28 games in the regular season, Kuzava retired Snider on a pop-up to third for out number two. Kuzava now faced dangerous clutch hitter Jackie Robinson, who swung at a three and two pitch and lofted a little fly ball between the pitcher's mound and first. The hearts of Yankee fans stopped as first baseman Joe Collins and pitcher Kuzava stared at each other and did not make a move. Suddenly, two Dodgers were across the plate and another was rounding third. Hank Bauer recalled what happened next:

> From nowhere Billy Martin, our second baseman, came racing across the infield. Billy charged in like a runaway truck, holding his glove out. He lunged forward at the last second and the ball fell into his glove, about six inches off the ground. I still don't know how he got there that fast. But we knew that nothing the Dodgers did after that could keep us from winning.[12]

Sure enough, Kuzava set the Dodgers down in the eighth and the ninth. The New York Yankees were world champions—again.

# CHAPTER SIX

# *P*ower, Speed, and Soul: The Slow Reintegration of Baseball

The theory behind Branch Rickey's "Great Experiment" was that after major-league owners, players, and fans saw with their own eyes that an African-American player could play in the National League and help his team win—without provoking race riots in the stands or racial violence on the field—then the color line would collapse under its own weight. Organized baseball had always used two rationalizations to justify excluding African-Americans and dark-skinned Hispanic players: they were not good enough to compete, and bigoted teammates and fans would never accept their presence. By the year 1950, however, the examples of Jackie Robinson, Larry Doby, Roy Campanella, Satchel Paige, Monte Irvin, Minnie Minoso, and Don Newcombe had pretty much settled the question of whether minority players could compete, and no race riots had been caused by anything that happened in a baseball game. Major-league baseball should have opened its doors wide to the hundreds of qualified minority players who were out there; instead, the integration process proceeded painfully slowly.

It was as if the major league clubs could not completely let go of the idea of the color line. For years after Jackie Robinson broke in with the Dodgers in 1947 and Cleveland's Larry Doby integrated the American League later in that same season, Bill Veeck, Branch Rickey, and a few other baseball men signed a few minority players here and there. Many clubs refused to sign any at all. With all the experienced Negro League players who were eager to come to the majors and all the young, unsigned African-American and Hispanic prospects across the country and in the Caribbean, the sixteen major league clubs signed a grand total of only two minority players in 1948, four in 1949, one in 1950, and eight in 1951.

It took the New York Yankees until 1955 to sign their first African-American player, catcher Elston Howard. The Phillies, Tigers, Red Sox, and Cardinals made no effort at all to sign minority players until the very end of the decade. For the entire decade of the 1950s, an average of about 8 percent of major leaguers were African-Americans. Today, not counting dark-skinned Hispanics, who would also have been excluded under the pre-1947 color line, African-Americans hold about 25 percent of all major-league jobs. As Bill James has pointed out, there were more players of Polish descent in 1950s baseball than African-Americans. Why would baseball owners and executives refuse to hire players who could help their teams win? With the old rationalizations for excluding African-Americans stripped away, only one explanation remains— the personal racism of those who ran baseball. Perhaps that had been the real reason behind the baseball color line all along.

The strange thing about the reintegration of baseball that continued throughout the 1950s and stretched well into the 1960s is that after Jackie Robinson, baseball clubs raised rather than lowered the bar for potential minority major leaguers. The powers that ran major-league baseball had grown tired of the tongue-lashings meted out by Robinson, who never stopped crusading for better treat-

*The New York Giants' Monte Irvin, Willie Mays, and Hank Thompson pose before a game. Despite the presence of such African-American stars as Jackie Robinson, Roy Campanella, and Mays, the integration of baseball proceeded slowly throughout the 1950s.*

ment for himself and his fellow minority players. Robinson was branded a hothead and a rabble-rouser simply for speaking obvious truths. When he accused the New York Yankees of racism on national television, he was criticized from one end of the country to the other. How did he know the motives or psychology of the men who ran the Yankees? "If the Yankees were so concerned," Robinson replied, "why didn't they answer in the only convincing way they could, by hiring some black players?"

Branch Rickey had wanted a clean-cut, educated, and responsible man to carry the burden of being first across the color line, but he also wanted a man who was tough and a fighter, both on the field and off. After seeing Robinson, Rickey's fellow owners decided they preferred someone more like Roy Campanella, a happy-go-lucky type who was grateful for being allowed to play in the majors and was reluctant to rock the boat. It was not enough to be a good or even a great player, the African-Americans and Hispanics who came after Robinson had to be politically docile, clean-cut, and conservative on racial issues. Personal failings that were tolerated in white players, such as alcoholism, womanizing, and gambling, disqualified many African-American prospects from consideration. Players were blacklisted for dating white women. The terms scouts and general managers used when they recommended a minority player in their scouting reports included "gentleman," "well-mannered," "articulate," and "not too black."

This is not to say that all the minority players of the 1950s were timid Uncle Toms—no one would say that about Frank Robinson or Hank Aaron—but baseball fans would have to wait another fifteen or twenty years before they would see an African-American player as outspoken about race or politics as a Jackie Robinson or a Satchel Paige.

## THE YEAR: 1957

Casey Stengel guided the Yankees to his customary 98 wins and the AL pennant despite playing a 41-year-old, Enos "Country" Slaughter, in left and bringing along a new double-play combination of 21-year-old second baseman Bobby Richardson and 20-year-old shortstop Tony Kubek. As usual, Stengel kept plenty of valuable backups around, including first baseman–catcher-outfielder Elston Howard and utility man Jerry Coleman. Skowron, McDougald, and Berra all had productive offensive seasons. Mantle followed up his 1955 tour de force with another MVP-winning performance. He batted .365, stole 16 bases, hit 34 homers, and scored a league-leading 121 runs. Al Lopez's Chicago White Sox tried to use speedsters Luis Aparicio and Minnie Minoso to run away with the AL race, but the team faded late and came in eight games back. Boston's 38-year-old Ted Williams became the oldest man to win a batting title, hitting .388 for the third-place Red Sox. Washington's Roy Sievers led in homers with 42 and RBIs with 114. New York Yankees left-hander Bobby Shantz beat out staffmate Tom Sturdivant to take the AL ERA title at 2.45.

In the NL, the Milwaukee Braves finally put it all together and easily beat out the Cardinals and Dodgers. The Milwaukee offense got big home-run seasons from third baseman Eddie Mathews, outfielder Wes Covington, and MVP Hank Aaron, who batted .322—tied with Frank Robinson for third after batting champion Stan Musial at .351 and Willie Mays at .333—and led the NL in homers with 44 and RBIs with 132. Cy Young winner Warren Spahn, Lew Burdette, and Bob Buhl paced the Braves' pitching staff, going a combined 56–27. Johnny Podres of Brooklyn won the ERA title at 2.66. In October, the Braves edged out New York in a seven game World Series. The big heroes were Hank Aaron, who batted .393, and Lew Burdette, who won all three of his starts. The 1957 season also saw a scandal in the All-Star game balloting, as Cincinnati Reds fans stuffed the ballot box and elected a team of nine Reds as the NL starters. As a result, the right to vote for All-Stars was taken away from fans, and for the next few years, players themselves made the selections.

As the 1950s wore on, African-American and dark-skinned Hispanic players persevered and fought their way through the obstacle course that the baseball establishment had set in their path. It was not easy. There were a hundred more Jackie Robinsons and Larry Dobys, African-American players who had to be the first to integrate various minor-league clubs, leagues, and classifications. Most of them experienced terrible loneliness and were reviled by fans, ignored and misunderstood by callow white teammates, and left to fend for themselves by their employers. Years and in some cases decades would pass, for instance, before major-league clubs would insist that their players be housed in integrated hotels. Until then African-American players often ate in different restaurants and stayed at different hotels from their teammates. This was particularly true in the south—but not exclusively. As late as the late 1950s, many major-league clubs put their white players up in segregated hotels in cities like St. Louis, Philadelphia, and Baltimore.

Slowly but surely, however, minority players trickled into the big leagues and not only survived, but succeeded beyond Branch Rickey's wildest dreams. By the end of the decade, enough African-Americans had crossed the color line that the style of play in the major leagues, especially in the NL, began to change. Before the integration of baseball, the all-white major leagues played a plodding, wait-for-the-home-run game. With the frequent exception of the three New York teams, managers discouraged the running game and played a monotonous brand of baseball that stressed conserving outs and base runners until the inevitable home run came along to drive everybody in. Watching major-league baseball in the early 1950s was like watching a blasting area at a big construction site; most of the time very little happened, but every once in a while there would be a big bang.

The Negro Leagues, on the other hand, played a much more exciting game that featured the hit and run, bunt plays, and lots of base stealing to put pressure on opposing defenses even when the home-run hitters were not doing their job. The several dozen African-American players who followed Jackie Robinson into the big leagues brought this style of play with them. As the major leagues—the NL, in particular—fielded more and more African-American stars who could run and hit for power, the Negro League style became the major-league style. The stage was set for the 1960s, a decade in which base-stealing would make a comeback and in which African-American superstars and their teams would dominate.

The pioneers in this process were mostly outfielders. Some of them had outstanding speed; others had outstanding power. The vast majority of them had plenty of both. A few of the first and the greatest are profiled below.

Cuban-born Saturnino Orestes Arrieta Armas Minoso, who, thankfully, was willing to answer to "Minnie," was one of the many dark-skinned Caribbean players of the 1950s who would have been relegated to the Negro Leagues had he come to the United States before Jackie Robinson. Minoso is remembered mostly for his speed and ability to hit for average, but he had decent power. Playing mostly for the White Sox, he led the AL in doubles once and triples three times, while hitting 15 to 25 home runs a season in his prime. A hustling player who played the game with an exuberance that could be felt by the fans in the stands, Minoso was extremely popular everywhere he went. Chicago fans loved to watch him run. In 1951, his first year with the White Sox, the fans chanted, "Go, Minnie, go!" whenever he got on base, and they were rarely disappointed. Minoso finished the season with 14 triples and 31 stolen bases, both league-leading figures. Like most of his fellow racial pioneers, Minoso was thrown at by opposing pitchers in an attempt to intimidate him. In 1956 he broke the major-league record of 21 times hit by a pitch. His inevitable reaction was to smile, toss the baseball back to the pitcher, and jog down to first base as though nothing had happened. "It was an accident every time," Minoso once said wryly. "I have been hit in the head eight times. But I would rather die than stop playing."

Willie Mays came up with the New York Giants in 1951 but established himself in 1954 with a .345, 87 extra-base-hit season that put him in a class with the best the major leagues had to offer. It was as if the baseball gods had put all of the baseball skills that ever were—even those that had fallen into disuse in the white major leagues—into one person. Born in Alabama, Mays signed with the Birmingham Black Barons of the Negro American League in 1948, when he was 17. The Giants discovered him by accident while looking at another player; three years later he was leading the International League, one of baseball's top minor leagues, in batting at .477. He finished the 1951 season with the Giants; trivia buffs will remember that a jittery Mays was waiting in the on-deck circle when Bobby Thomson hit the home run that won the 1951 pennant.

A once-in-a-generation kind of ballplayer, Willie Mays made everyone happy: his teammates, the fans, the sportswriters—even some of those who were less than enthusiastic about the integration of baseball. Mays was no Jackie Robinson. He never went to college and had little to say about political or social issues. What he did do was play baseball with so much skill, heart, and beauty that, as Larry Moffi and Jonathan Kronstadt have written, "Jackie Robinson won the respect of baseball fans, black and white, [but] Willie Mays won their hearts." He had the power and speed of a Mickey Mantle but didn't drink, and he kept himself in splendid shape. Mays hit well enough to win an NL batting title and finish his 22-year career with a .302 lifetime average; he had enough power to reach the 50-homer mark twice and hit 660 for his career, third on the all-time list behind Babe Ruth and Hank Aaron; and he ran well enough to hit 140 triples and steal 338 bases.

Mays also played center field like a dream, covering amazing amounts of ground, catching the ball with his hands waist-high—his trademark basket catch—and treating Giants fans to one great circus catch after another, many of them followed up by even more astounding throws. In the 1954 World Series, Mays sprinted, his back to the infield, to a point 450 feet from home plate and caught a Vic Wertz drive over his shoulder on the dead run; he then whirled and fired a bullet back to the infield that kept the Indians base runners from tagging up and advancing. The Giants won the game in extra innings. Partly because it was televised, that was Mays's most celebrated catch, but New York Giants fans could remember seeing half a dozen that were better. As writer William Goldman described the first time he saw Mays play:

> I fell in love with him that afternoon. And watching him then, I realized unconsciously that it was about time he arrived on my horizon, because during all those years of being bored by baseball, of sitting in bleacher seats for pitcher's battles, or dying with the heat while the manager brought in some slow reliever, I'd been waiting for Willie.
>
> He was what it was all about. He was the reason. In my head, there was a notion of the way things ought to happen, but never quite do. Not until Willie came along. And then I could finally sit there and say to myself, Oh sure, that's it.[1]

Ernie Banks came over to the Chicago Cubs from the Negro League Kansas City Monarchs in 1953. Another African-American star who steered clear of politics—"The only race we have in baseball," he liked to say, "is the run to beat the throw"—Banks treated racist insults, segregated hotels, and the inevitable mailed death threats with the same indifference that he displayed to opposing pitchers who threw at his head. Banks did not let anything interfere with his game, which was playing a great shortstop and hitting the long ball. Between 1954 and 1962, Banks frequently led the NL in two of the three Triple Crown stats, racking up home-run totals of 19, 44, 28, 43, 47, 45, 41, 29, and 37. After leg injuries forced him to move to first base in 1962, Banks's performance dropped a notch, but he continued to produce 20- to 30-homer seasons and drive in 80 to 100 runs almost every year for another ten seasons. One of Chicago's most popular living athletes, Ernie Banks retired with 512 home runs and 2,583 career base hits.

As Hank Aaron learned, even a quarter-century after Jackie Robinson broke the color line, race still mattered in major-league baseball. In 1973 Aaron was on the down side of a brilliant career, but what a down side it was! One of the most consistent sluggers in baseball history, Aaron had hit between 24 and 47 home runs every season since 1955. He had won four home-run titles and matched his uniform number by hitting 44 home runs in four different seasons. Now 37 years old, Hank Aaron was closing in on Babe Ruth's career mark of 714 homers, a record that few had expected ever to be reached or even seriously challenged. The two men had little in common. A flamboyant, heavy-drinking, big-eating, overgrown adolescent, Ruth had produced most of his home runs in a 14-year period punctuated by outbursts of 54, 59, 60, and 54 home runs in a season; in between these big years Ruth's long-ball totals would sometimes slip into the 30s or even the 20s. Ruth enjoyed the advantages of being left-handed and playing in an era when the competitive balance between offense and defense was tilted toward the hitters.

Aaron, on the other hand, took excellent care of his body. Unlike Ruth, Aaron ran well and played a superb defensive outfield for most of his 23-year career. Hank Aaron played under the disadvantages of hitting right-handed and playing most of his career in the 1960s, a baseball era dominated by overpowering pitchers like Bob Gibson, Juan Marichal, Sandy Koufax, and Don Drysdale. It is difficult to imagine how a player could hit 700 home runs under these conditions. He could average 70 homers a year for 10 years, or 35 for 20 years, or 17.5 a year for 40 years. Any way you figure it, it seems unlikely. To do it, as Aaron did, without ever hitting more than 47 in any one season, seems impossible.

Aaron entered the 1973 season needing 41 homers to

*Hank Aaron practices his swing before a Braves'
game. The slugger won four home-run titles in his
23-year career and broke Babe Ruth's career mark
of 714 homers in 1974.*

tie Ruth's record and 42 to become the major leagues' all-time career home run leader. That is when the death threats and the hate mail started to arrive. Even after Robinson and Banks and Mays and Minoso, there was still a small minority of white fans who could not handle the idea of Babe Ruth being pushed out of the record books by an African-American. Not that the quiet but deadly serious Aaron was going to let any of that bother him. "I came to the Braves on business," Aaron later said, "and I intended to see that business was good as long as I could." He finished the 1973 season one shy of Ruth's record but made up for it on his first swing of 1974, when he launched a pitch from Dodgers pitcher Al Downing into the visitors bullpen. Aaron retired in 1976 with a .305 lifetime batting average and 755 career homers.

As the Negro Leagues withered and died in the mid-1950s, major-league clubs began to look elsewhere for African-American players. Frank Robinson, who debuted with the Cincinnati Reds in 1956, was among the first of a new generation of minority stars who came up through the formerly all-white minors rather than from the Negro Leagues. A native of Oakland, California, Robinson once made the astounding and, to a baseball fan, sad statement that "I didn't know anything about racism or bigotry until I went into professional baseball in 1953." When the Reds sent him to a Columbia, South Carolina, club that had never before had an African-American player, he got a crash course in Jim Crow.

In spite of the racial heckling from the fans, the insults from other players, and the bladder-busting long bus trips with rest stops at whites-only restaurants, Robinson played well. "Have a good year, and get out of here," he repeated to himself like a mantra. He made the big club by 1956. In his rookie season, the 20-year-old Robinson hit .290, stole 8 bases, hit 38 home runs, and won the NL Rookie of the Year award. Over the next ten years, the hustling, hard-sliding slugger gained a reputation for playing hard but clean baseball. He produced several near-Triple Crown seasons before leading the Reds to a pennant in 1961 and winning the MVP.

Traded to Baltimore in 1966, Robinson won the Triple Crown, batting .316 with 49 homers and 122 RBIs, and became the first man in history to win the MVP award in both leagues. He went on to lead the Orioles to four World Series. After retiring with 586 career homers and a .294 lifetime batting average, Frank Robinson became the first African-American to manage a major-league team. He is currently a baseball executive.

The statistical record of major-league baseball in the 1950s amply demonstrates the criminally slow pace of baseball's integration, or, to those who know the whole story of race and professional baseball, its re-integration. After Jackie Robinson and the rest of the first five minority players crossed the color line in 1947, only two more came in 1948. The class of 1949 consisted of eleven men and the class of 1950 only twelve. Not all of these players, of course, stuck in the majors. Baseball was employing a classic pattern of discrimination, following an unofficial policy of tolerating minority players only if they were stars or superstars. Nothing makes this point better than the voting results for the MVP and Rookie of the Year awards, and the seasonal leaders in the major offensive categories. Consider the fact that in the 1950s, on average, no more than three dozen of the major leagues' four hundred or so playing jobs were held by African-American or dark-skinned Hispanic players. Then look at the seasonal leaders in the three Triple Crown categories—batting average, home runs, and RBIs—plus stolen bases. For each category, there are a possible 20 seasonal leaders. Twelve times in the 1950s minority players lead their league in stolen bases. The rest of the figures are batting average, three times; home runs, five times; and RBIs, seven times. The awards results are even more striking: eight minority players won MVP awards in the 1950s, and seven were named Rookie of the Year.

These numbers tell us one more thing: that the NL was much quicker to integrate than the AL, and more affected by the trend toward power-and-speed style baseball. Of the 1950s' twelve stolen base leaders, only three were American Leaguers. Of the three batting champions, none played in the AL. Of the five home-run leaders, two played in the AL. And of the seven RBI leaders, only two were from the AL. In fact, if you take away Larry Doby and Minnie Minoso, there is not one AL player on any of the lists. Meanwhile the NL boasted perennial all-stars like Sam Jethroe, Billy Bruton, Monte Irvin, Ernie Banks, Mays, Aaron, and Campanella. As for the awards, minority players won the NL MVP in 1951, 1953, 1954, 1955, 1956, 1957, 1958, and 1959; they won the Rookie of the Year in 1950, 1951, 1952, 1953, 1956, 1958, and 1959. No minority player won the AL version of either award once.

# CHAPTER SEVEN

# California Dreamin':
# The Era of Franchise Shifts

Different historians have come up with different explanations for the business slump that baseball experienced during the 1950s, a decade of booming economic expansion for most other industries. Some blame it on the movement of the middle class into the suburbs and the subsequent decay of the inner city. One problem with this theory is that no minor-league or major-league franchises relocated to take advantage of the growing, suburban market. The suburbs were, and remain today, a professional baseball wasteland. Another is that the minor leagues, most of whose clubs were located in small cities and towns, suffered even more than the majors during the 1950s. Some blame it on television, saying that the fans of the 1950s preferred to watch ballgames in the comfort of their homes, but today television promotes rather than hurts ticket sales at major-league ballparks. Still others have blamed baseball's downturn in the 1950s on boredom with the New York Yankees' monopoly on the AL pennant and the World Series. If that is so, then what explains the baseball boom of the 1920s, a decade thoroughly dominated by the teams of Babe Ruth and Lou Gehrig?

The real explanation for baseball's decline in the 1950s is probably a combination of two things: one, boredom and disenchantment with baseball's monotonous style of play and its crumbling, 1900s- and 1910s-era facilities; and two, baseball's stubborn refusal to respond to the movement of America's population center, which had been shifting westward and southward for decades.

As baseball history well demonstrates, this failure is a by-product of baseball's monopolistic structure. Expansion means more money for the industry as a whole, but it also means letting new investors into the monopoly club. And that would mean sharing power with more owners. The men who run baseball have always preferred a bigger piece of a smaller pie to a smaller piece of a much larger pie, even if it means lower overall profits. The bottom line is that any industry needs to keep up with the times and to improve its product and its methods of marketing constantly. In 1952, major-league baseball was being played in the same northeastern cities as in 1903 and in many of the same ballparks as in the 1910s. Baseball was falling hopelessly behind the times.

Consider the minor leagues. Going back to the late 19th century, the major-league owners had tried to dominate the minors. By the 1930s they had succeeded in turning nearly every minor-league club from an independent, competitive entertainment business into a subsidiary of a major-league club. The purpose of the minors changed from winning championships and selling tickets to serving as schools for major-league prospects. The interests of local fans were strictly secondary to those of the organization. Inevitably, in the vast parts of the United States where there was no major-league franchise, sports fans turned away from baseball and toward college sports, basketball, and football. All of these offered fans real competition;

there was no "parent club" to steal away a team's biggest star in the middle of playoffs or in the final weeks of a pennant race.

There were exceptions to this trend, of course. One of them was the Pacific Coast League, which operated in huge markets such as Los Angeles and San Francisco, and many of whose franchises made enough money to compete with the major leagues for middle and lower-level playing talent. As the events of the late 1950s and 1960s would demonstrate, the baseball monopoly would find a way to take minimum economic advantage of that situation.

A classic characteristic of monopolies is that they are overconservative, making changes only when they are desperate. This is the main reason that as the 1950s began, no major-league baseball was played south of Washington, D.C., or west of St. Louis, Missouri. Meanwhile, St. Louis, Chicago, Boston, and Philadelphia each had two major-league franchises. New York City had three. In 1953, the owners of the St. Louis Browns and the Boston Braves were desperate. A baseball disaster area, the perennially cellar-dwelling Browns had tried and failed to move their franchise to the west coast before the war. In 1951, brilliant baseball promoter Bill Veeck gave AL baseball in St. Louis one last try. He bought the Browns and pulled out all the promotional stops. He pinch-hit a midget for laughs. He hired big-name talent like pitcher Satchel Paige and manager Rogers Hornsby. The ancient Paige was a success, going 12–10 with 10 saves and a 3.07 ERA in 1952. The opinionated, acid-tongued Hornsby, however, gave Veeck as much trouble as he had given Veeck's father when he had briefly managed the Chicago Cubs in the early 1930s. Veeck Jr. fired Hornsby 50 games into the 1952 season.

In the end, nothing Veeck did could change the basic economics of the situation. The Browns, who had been drawing around 250,000 fans per season, doubled their attendance in 1952 but fell back to under 300,000 in

1953. Out of ideas, Veeck tried to get permission from the other owners to move the club to Baltimore, a solid minor-league town, but he was so unpopular among his fellow owners that he was turned down. As a result, Veeck ran out of cash and was forced to sell the team. Meanwhile, Boston Braves owner Lou Perini transferred his chronically poor-drawing club to Milwaukee. The following year, Veeck's successors were given the green light to go to Baltimore.

Both clubs got new, publicly built stadiums and huge attendance increases. The Braves translated box office gains into on-field championships almost immediately. In 1954 the Browns, now playing under the name Baltimore Orioles, drew a respectable 850,000 fans despite finishing seventh and losing 100 games. The Orioles took a little longer than the Braves to become competitive, but they climbed into the first division by the early 1960s and emerged as baseball's best team toward the end of the decade.

In 1955 the Philadelphia Athletics, another baseball slum, relocated to a brand-new stadium in Kansas City. Even though they finished in sixth place, the club drew 1.3 million, second in the AL only to the pennant-winning New York Yankees. All three moves were such successes, at least in the short-term, that almost every major-league owner began to see franchise relocation as the answer to his problems.

Two men who were watching these events very closely were Brooklyn Dodgers owner Walter O'Malley and New York Giants owner Horace Stoneham. Both were unhappy with their attendance, although the Giants had a bigger problem. Both franchises occupied decaying, outmoded ballparks, and both were tired of playing second fiddle to the number one team in baseball, the New York Yankees. After the A's move in 1955, O'Malley began talking publicly about the necessity of moving unless he got a new ballpark in Brooklyn. To create a sense of urgency, he even scheduled a few Dodgers home games in an abandoned minor-league park in Jersey City, New Jersey. The next few years went by, however, without any significant action from New York City or New York State officials.

Meanwhile, tiny Ebbets Field continued to deteriorate, and the Giants' attendance dropped each year. It declined steadily from over one million in 1950 to barely 629,000 in 1956. Then an event occurred completely outside of baseball that started Walter O'Malley thinking: the aircraft manufacturer Boeing brought out the 707, a commercial jet that flew faster and carried more passengers than any previous airliner. The 707 could fly from the east coast to the west coast in six hours. That meant that a baseball team could travel from Los Angeles to New York in one off-day, in fact, it could do so using less time than it had once taken big-league clubs to travel from New York to St. Louis by train.

Casting an envious eye on the growing Los Angeles market, O'Malley held meetings with Los Angeles politicians. He was offered Chavez Ravine, a 300-acre piece of land in downtown Los Angeles, as a ballpark site. Most significantly, he swapped the Dodgers' minor-league franchise in Fort Worth, Texas, for the Chicago Cubs' PCL franchise, the Los Angeles Angels. Now that he controlled the baseball rights to part of the Los Angeles market—those of the PCL Hollywood Stars would be bought later by the AL California Angels—the only thing that could stop him was his fellow owners. A shrewd politician, O'Malley had already locked up the necessary votes. After the 1957 season, O'Malley made public his decision to go. In order to meet potential objections over how this would disrupt the NL schedule, he talked Stoneham into moving the Giants to San Francisco. It was not difficult. By the opening of the 1958 season, both teams were occupying former minor-league parks in California. Both had been promised new ballparks, courtesy of California taxpayers.

112

*Following a 9-1 loss to the Pirates on September 29, 1957, Giants players dash toward their clubhouse ahead of fans. It was the last game that the Giants played at the Polo Grounds before moving to San Francisco.*

## THE YEAR: 1958

Both the Dodgers and the Giants were box-office successes in their first season on the west coast. When the two clubs played each other on Opening Day in Los Angeles, a record crowd of over 78,000 filled the monstrous Los Angeles Coliseum. Ill-suited for baseball, the Coliseum featured an extremely short left-field wall topped by a 40-foot screen and a 440-foot power alley in right-center that would neutralize the power of Duke Snider. Neither team was heard from in the NL pennant race, as the Giants finished third and the Dodgers seventh. Once again Mathews, Covington, and Aaron provided the offense, and 20-game-winners Warren Spahn and Lew Burdette led a fine young pitching staff as the Braves won the NL flag by eight games over a youthful Pirates club. Philadelphia's Richie Ashburn won the batting title at .350, and Chicago's Ernie Banks won the MVP and led in home runs with 47 and RBIs with 129. San Francisco's diminutive change-up artist, Stu Miller, took the ERA title at 2.47.

The Yankees thoroughly dominated the AL race, winning over Chicago by ten games. Mickey Mantle batted .304 with a league-high 42 homers and 97 RBIs. Every other member of the Yankees regular lineup reached double figures in homers, with the exception of shortstop Kubek. Cy Young winner Bob Turley led the AL in wins, going 21–7, and Whitey Ford won the league ERA title at 2.01. New York led the AL in runs, home runs, batting average, double plays, shutouts, saves, and team ERA. Ted Williams won his sixth and final batting title at .328, and teammate and MVP Jackie Jensen led the AL in RBIs with 122. In the World Series, Stengel's club dropped three of the first four games but rallied to defeat Milwaukee in seven.

There was no big outcry about the departure of the New York Giants. As a franchise that had long competed for the same fans as the New York Yankees, they were more or less a lost cause long before 1957. Before O'Malley sold him on California, owner Horace Stoneham was already preparing to relocate to Minneapolis, where he owned the minor-league franchise. As it dawned on Brooklyn fans that they were about to lose their team, however, they signed petitions, wrote letters, and pressured their politicians to do something. The idea that the Dodgers might leave Brooklyn was met with a combination of horror and disbelief.

According to the most powerful politicians of the day, New York City mayor Robert Wagner and parks commissioner Robert Moses, nothing they could have done would have kept O'Malley from moving the Dodgers out of Brooklyn. Still, some blame these two for not coming up with a publicly-financed stadium attractive enough to keep the Dodgers from going to California. The vast majority of Brooklynites, however, saw the Dodgers' move as a terrible and unjustifiable betrayal by one man—Walter O'Malley. There is a story that sums up how many people in New York and Brooklyn still feel about him. One night writers Jack Newfield and Pete Hamill decided to write down the names of the three worst human beings who ever lived and then compare their two lists. "Each of us," Newfield recalled, "wrote down the same three names and in the same order: Hitler, Stalin, Walter O'Malley."

The wounds left by the departure of the Dodgers have never completely healed. To this day, many former Brooklyn Dodger fans are so bitter that they cannot bring themselves to root for any baseball team at all. A few years ago, Los Angeles Dodgers owner Peter O'Malley, the son of Walter, infuriated millions of New Yorkers by suing to stop a Bay Ridge, Brooklyn, sports bar from calling itself "The Brooklyn Dodger." O'Malley's lawyers claimed that they owned all rights to that name. For a borough whose citizens had earned the nickname "trolley dodgers" by decades of evading the streetcars that once ran up and down the long, flat streets of Brooklyn, and who had rooted for the Dodgers from the days of Ned Hanlon through the lean Uncle Robby years to the great dynasty of the 1950s, this was too much. As a headline in the New York *Daily News* put it: "O'Malley Sticks It to Brooklyn Again."

# THE YEAR: 1959

NL fans enjoyed a thrilling, three-team race between the up-and-coming San Francisco Giants of Willie Mays,

Orlando Cepeda, Sam Jones, and Johnny Antonelli; the revived Los Angeles Dodgers of Don Drysdale, Wally Moon, Maury Wills, and Charlie Neal; and the Milwaukee Braves. Going into the season's final week leading the Braves and Dodgers by two games, the Giants dropped out of contention by losing three in a row to Los Angeles, who finished the season tied with the Braves. Playing in their third post-season pennant playoff series, the Dodgers swept Milwaukee, two games to none. Hank Aaron won the 1959 NL batting title with a .355 average; teammate Eddie Mathews led in homers with 46; and MVP Ernie Banks repeated as RBI champion. Sam Jones and fellow Giant Stu Miller were one and two in ERA at 2.83 and 2.84; they were followed closely by Milwaukee's starting tandem of Bob Buhl at 2.86 and Warren Spahn at 2.96.

In the AL, slumps from several key players dropped the Yankees into last place early. The club bounced back, but finished third to Al Lopez's "Go-Go" Sox, a team with little power but lots of speed, and the second-place Cleveland Indians. White Sox second baseman Nellie Fox won the MVP award, and teammate Early Wynn the Cy Young. The World Series illustrated the old baseball adage that the running game only works against bad teams; shut down on the basepaths by Los Angeles catcher John Roseboro, the White Sox went down in six games.

As for the effect of the Dodgers' and Giants' move to California on baseball, in the short-term both franchises improved their attendance and financial health, although the Los Angeles Dodgers got a better ballpark out of the deal and have always been far more profitable than the Giants. In the long-term, however, it created problems for baseball as a whole that have been partially redressed only by expansion, or the addition of new franchises to each league. Looking back, it probably would have been better for baseball if the Pacific Coast League had been admitted, in one form or another, as a third major league in the late

1950s. Instead, one of baseball's strongest minor leagues was virtually destroyed by having its two biggest markets stolen by the NL. In the end, of course, PCL cities such as Seattle, Oakland, and San Diego have been admitted to the major leagues anyway, through a chaotic process of relocation and expansion that lasted decades. The other negative result of Walter O'Malley's scheme was to take a natural two-team market with three teams, New York City, and turn it into a two-team market with only one team. The loss of the Giants and Dodgers did not help the Yankees, but it did leave millions of NL fans with no team to follow until the expansion of 1962 brought the New York Mets to Queens.

# M and M: Mantle and Maris and the Race Against Ruth

In 1960 the Yankees rebounded from a third-place finish to win their tenth AL pennant under Casey Stengel. The team then lost the World Series to the Pittsburgh Pirates, a clearly inferior team, in the most disheartening way possible. The powerful Yankee lineup scored 55 runs to Pittsburgh's 27 yet lost, four games to three. It was probably just bad luck, but some blamed Casey Stengel. In particular the Yankee manager was second-guessed for giving pitcher Art Ditmar the start in game one, which meant that staff ace Whitey Ford pitched twice instead of three times in the series. Ford pitched complete-game shutouts in both of his starts; Ditmar went 0–2 with an ERA of 21.60. There were also whispers that Stengel, who had turned 70 during the summer, was getting old and losing his young team emotionally. Five days after the end of the World Series, the Yankees held a press conference to announce that Stengel had resigned because of age and that coach Ralph Houk would be taking his place. Popular with the Yankees players, Houk lacked Casey Stengel's ability to charm the press.

Under questioning from skeptical reporters, a bitter but

controlled Stengel made it clear that he had been fired. "I'll never make the mistake of being seventy again," was his best line. Two weeks later, the shakeup continued, and George Weiss was also out. No one knew it at the time, but neither Weiss nor Stengel was through with baseball yet. The two men would soon join forces with another spurned baseball party—New York's Dodgers and Giants fans—to make one of baseball history's most unlikely comebacks.

The club of 1961 was a classic example of the deep Yankee organization's ability to rebuild on the fly. Other than veterans Moose Skowron, Yogi Berra, and Whitey Ford, the team consisted mostly of 25-year-olds. Shortstop Tony Kubek, second baseman Bobby Richardson, third baseman Clete Boyer, right fielder Roger Maris, pitcher Ralph Terry, pitcher Bill Stafford, and pitcher Rollie Sheldon, all regulars, ranged between 24 and 26. Team leader Mickey Mantle may have been a ten-year veteran, but he was still only 29. In 1960 this club had won 97 games under an increasingly crabby and sarcastic Stengel. The way it played a year later under the easygoing and personable Houk, however, suggests that the Yankees probably did the right thing by changing managers.

The 1961 Yankees went 109–53, steamrolling over the rest of the AL. Runner-up Detroit, a 101-game winner, finished eight games out. Armed with the power hitting of Roger Maris and Mickey Mantle; the defense of Berra, Boyer, Kubek, and Richardson; and the pitching of starters Whitey Ford and Bill Stafford, and reliever Luis Arroyo, the 1961 Yankees became one of the three or four teams that are always mentioned whenever baseball fans argue over which baseball team was the best of all time.

# THE YEAR: 1960

After being forced out of Brooklyn in 1950 by Walter O'Malley, Branch Rickey took over the Pittsburgh Pirates and began to rebuild that barren organization from the ground up. It took a while, but in 1960 Rickey's efforts bore their first fruit as a homegrown Pirates team of Roberto Clemente, Bill Mazeroski, Dick Groat, Don Hoak, Bob Skinner, Vernon Law, Bob Friend, and Roy Face took the NL flag by seven games over the Braves. Shortstop Groat and third baseman Hoak finished first and second in the MVP voting, and Law went 20–9 to win the Cy Young award. Groat won the batting title, hitting .325. San Francisco's Mike McCormick led the league in ERA at 2.70. Familiar names Ernie Banks and Hank Aaron led the NL in homers and RBIs, respectively.

A less than overpowering Yankee team won the AL flag by eight games over Baltimore, partly thanks to the trade that brought outfielder Roger Maris from Kansas City to New York. The left-handed hitting Maris swatted 39 home runs, drove in 112 runs—a league-high—and was voted AL MVP. Boston's Pete Runnels won the batting title with a .320 average and Chicago's Frank Baumann won the ERA title at 2.67. Mickey Mantle beat out Maris for the league lead in homers with 40. The Yankees dropped the World Series in seven games, despite convincing everybody outside of western Pennsylvania that they were the better team. New York won its three games by scores of 16-3, 10-0, and 12-0; Pittsburgh won its games by scores of 6-4, 3-2, 5-2, and 10-9.

The year 1960 also saw Reds reliever Jim Brosnan publish *The Long Season*, a personal memoir that gave readers an idea of what it was really like to be an ordinary player in the major leagues. With its refreshing frankness, the book violated many baseball taboos and established a precedent for the much more controversial and more famous *Ball Four*, Jim Bouton's journal of the 1969 season.

One thing that made the 1961 Yankees special was the home-run race against Babe Ruth's record of 60 home runs in a single season. Ruth set his mark with the Yankees in 1927. Other sluggers had taken aim at Ruth's record in the

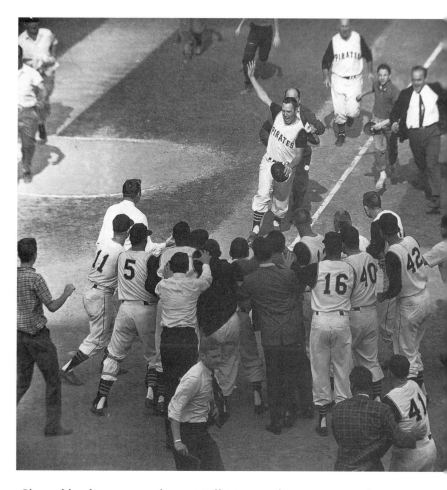

*Chased by fans, an exuberant Bill Mazeroski races toward home plate and his waiting teammates. His ninth-inning homer clinched the 1960 World Series for the Pirates.*

meantime—there was Hack Wilson in 1930, Jimmie Foxx in 1932, and Hank Greenberg in 1938—but 1961 was the first time that two players in the same season raced each other for a shot at the record. The two players were also teammates: Roger Maris and Mickey Mantle.

*On August 16, 1961, Yankees sluggers Roger Maris and
Mickey Mantle flank Claire Ruth. The Babe's widow
was at the game to watch the two young hitters chase
Ruth's single-season home-run record.*

Both began the season on fire. By July 1, Roger Maris
was five games ahead of Babe Ruth's 1927 pace with 28
home runs. That day Mantle hit two to raise his total to 27.
One month later, Maris was leading Mantle, 40–38; both
were now weeks ahead of Ruth's pace. Of course, it
should be remembered that dozens of players have kept up
with Babe Ruth's 1927 home-run pace for half, or even
three-quarters of a season. What separates the men from
the boys is the month of September, when Ruth quickened

his pace considerably, hitting a daunting 17 home runs. By mid-summer, everyone in baseball, and a considerable number of non-fans, were completely wrapped up in the race between the M and M boys, as Maris and Mantle were nicknamed. Both men were subjected to enormous media pressure. This affected Maris a lot more than it affected Mantle. For one thing Mantle was older; for another, he had already been through much of this when he hit 52 homers in 1956. Finally, even though both men were insecure country boys at heart, Mantle was protected and treated with something approaching hero worship by the New York press corps. Many reporters openly rooted for Mantle to break the record; it seemed like the logical next step for an all-time Yankee great who had won MVPs, World Series championships, and a Triple Crown.

Maris, on the other hand, was a newcomer to the Yankees with no credentials as a superstar. He had won the MVP in 1960, but before that his career consisted of three years with Cleveland and Kansas City in which he had hit a total of 58 home runs and batted in the middle .200s. Mickey Mantle had learned to handle national media pressure and the tedium of answering the same questions over and over again. Maris had not. On top of all that, underlying many reporter's questions was an unspoken message of disrespect: "Who are you to challenge one of the greatest records of all time?" As teammate Tom Tresh remembered,

> The press and the fans just ate up all his time. He was the first one in the locker room in the morning and the last one to leave. He had maybe thirty, forty sportswriters around his locker. Once he hit the clubhouse he had no privacy whatsoever. He started losing hair in the back of his head from nerves.[1]

To Maris's credit, none of this slowed down his home-run hitting. At the end of August he had 51 and Mantle had 48.

Now, not only was the press rooting for Mantle, so were the fans. Manager Houk got letters complaining that it was unfair for Maris to bat third every day and Mantle fourth. They asked that Houk switch them in the batting order so that Mantle would get better pitches to hit. While it is easy to overrate position in the lineup as a factor in hitting, one statistic shows that it clearly made a difference in 1961: with a switch-hitting power-hitter like Mantle batting behind him virtually every day of the 1961 season, Roger Maris was never intentionally walked—not once. This is unheard-of for a middle-of-the-order home-run hitter, much less one who is on his way to hitting 61 home runs.

Meanwhile, another controversy arose. Defenders of Babe Ruth, a surprisingly sizable faction, raised the question of what would happen if one of the "M and M boys" hit 61 home runs in the 162-game schedule that the AL used in 1961. Since Babe Ruth's record had been set when the league used a 154-game schedule, they complained that a modern player was, in effect, getting eight extra games in which to break the record. Baseball Commissioner Ford Frick, a close friend of the Ruth family who had once served as Babe Ruth's ghost writer, announced that in order to officially break Ruth's record, Maris or Mantle would have to do it in 154 games. If they did it in 155 or more, then the record books would contain a note to that effect. The public took this to mean that an "asterisk" would be placed in the record book next to Maris's or Mantle's record if it was set using more than 154 games.

Frick's ruling was both wrong-headed and absurd. First of all, there is no such thing as an official baseball record book. There are official statistics, but those are simply numbers; they contain no interpretations, notes, or asterisks of the kind Frick was talking about. Second, the baseball schedule has been lengthened or shortened many times in the course of major-league history. In order to be consistent, there are literally hundreds of other records that would have to be marked with a similar note or asterisk.

Finally, Frick's ruling only makes sense if you believe that those eight regular-season games are the most significant difference between the conditions Ruth played under in 1927 and those Mantle and Maris played under in 1961. How do you account for other important differences such as train travel versus air travel, the advent of specialized relief pitching, or the invention of the slider? The answer is that you do not. Record books are for numbers. Interpreting those numbers is another matter. An irritated Maris said it best in 1961, when someone asked him what he thought of Frick's ruling. "A season's a season," he muttered. The bottom line is that today, contrary to what many baseball fans believe, there is no note or asterisk next to Maris's 1961 home-run record. There never has been.

## THE YEAR: 1961

The AL expanded to ten teams in 1961, adding franchises in Los Angeles, the California Angels; and Washington, D.C., the Senators. At the same time, the original Senators franchise relocated to Minnesota and changed its name to the Minnesota Twins. The resultant addition of two good hitters' parks helped make 1961 a big home run year; the addition of two noncompetitive expansion teams made the great 1961 Yankees look even more dominating. New York finished eight games ahead of a Detroit Tigers club that put up a surprisingly good fight for most of the season, but 38 games ahead of seventh-place Minnesota and 47½ games ahead of Kansas City and Washington, who lost 100 games each and finished in a tie for last place. Tiger Norm Cash won the AL batting honors at .361; teammate Al Kaline was second at .324. Repeat MVP Roger Maris, of course, led in home runs with 61 and RBIs with 142. Whitey Ford won the Cy Young award. Washington's Dick Donovan took the ERA title at 2.40 despite compiling a record of only 10–10.

The Cincinnati Reds surprised everyone by putting on

a 21–7 kick to pass by the Dodgers and Giants in the season's final weeks. The Reds won the pennant in the still eight-team NL by four games. Managed by Fred Hutchinson, the club featured power hitters Gordy Coleman, Gene Freese, Vada Pinson, Wally Post, and team leader and MVP Frank Robinson. Pitcher Joey Jay went 21–10 to lead the pitching staff. Pittsburgh's rising Puerto Rican star Roberto Clemente—stolen by Branch Rickey from the Dodgers farm system—won the batting title over Pinson, .351 to .343. Giants first baseman Orlando Cepeda made it a Puerto Rican Triple Crown of sorts by leading in homers with 46 and RBIs with 142. Milwaukee's Warren Spahn beat out Cincinnati's Jim O'Toole for the ERA title, 3.02 to 3.10. The Yankees wiped out the Reds, four games to one, in the World Series, as backup catcher and pinch-hitter Johnny Blanchard homered twice and Whitey Ford went 2–0 . Ford broke Babe Ruth's ancient World Series pitching record of 29⅔ scoreless innings in a row; he recorded a series ERA of 0.00 over 32 innings.

Ty Cobb, one of the greatest base-stealers and hitters for average of all time, died of cancer at 74.

Mantle got hot in early August, and on August 11 he actually led Maris, 44 home runs to 42. "At that point," Mantle later recalled, "I really started thinking about Ruth's 17 in September. How the hell did he do that?" Maris then surged and on September 1 he led his teammate 51 to 48. Both men were still hitting; the difference was that Mickey Mantle was enjoying himself. Already moody and a bit of a loner by nature, Roger Maris was now in a permanent bad mood, tired of fans knocking on his wife's door at their home and tired of every word he said showing up on page one of the newspapers. His hair continued to fall out, and he developed a skin rash caused by nerves. The longer it continued, the more the record chase added to the pressure of playing in the major leagues. This pressure affected everyone who got near him. Opposing pitchers pitched him differently; umpires were jittery; fans booed when he walked and booed when he struck out—some even booed when he hit a homer. On September 10, Maris began to pull away from Mantle for good. With Maris three home runs ahead with 56, Mantle came down with a terrible cold and stopped hitting. "I'm finished," he said, "I hope Roger can do it." Sure enough, a weakened Mantle finished the season with 54.

Thanks to Ford Frick and the "asterisk" dispute, Roger Maris's record chase ended with something of an anticlimax. Going into game number 154—played, appropriately enough, in Babe Ruth's birthplace of Baltimore—Maris had 58 home runs. He needed two to tie Ruth's record in 154 games, but he fell one short. On September 26, facing Orioles pitcher Jack Fisher at home, Maris hit a hanging curve ball out of the park for number 60. After the game, Claire Ruth congratulated Maris and said, "I know that if the Babe were here, he would have wanted to congratulate you." Maris replied, "I'm glad I didn't tie the Babe's record in 154 games. That is enough for me." When Roger Maris finally did get homer number 61, in the fourth inning of the final game of the season, there was some confusion about whether something truly historic had happened. You would certainly never have known from the next day's newspaper: "Baseball has two home-run kings today—the fabled Babe Ruth and a modern-day counterpart, Roger Maris" is how the Associated Press played it. As a result, when Maris set the all-time record for most home runs in a season by driving a low fastball from Red Sox pitcher Tracy Stallard into the lower-right field stands, only 25,000 fans were watching.

Strangely enough, Roger Maris's record has grown in stature as the decades have gone by. One obvious reason is that no one has broken it; Maris's record has now lasted 35 years—longer than Babe Ruth's did. Another reason is that the whole asterisk controversy has, thankfully, begun to fade from popular memory. Finally, in spite of his failure

*Roger Maris takes an uppercut swing at a pitch. By hitting 61 home runs in 1961, Maris eclipsed the single-season record of 60, which Babe Ruth set in 1927.*

to reach the Hall of Fame, Roger Maris's reputation is greater today than it was in 1961. Far from being a "bush leaguer" as Rogers Hornsby called him in 1961, Roger Maris was a multitalented ballplayer who hit with consistent power, ran the bases well, and played a splendid defensive right field. He won the MVP award twice. Above all, Maris was a winner. Even though his career lasted only 12 years, he played on seven pennant winners. He won five with New York. After Maris was traded to the St. Louis Cardinals in 1967, the Cardinals won NL flags in 1967 and in 1968. He must have been doing something right.

# CHAPTER NINE

# Amazin': The Underdog Expansion Mets

After the Dodgers and Giants left town in 1958, a group of lawyers, politicians, and wealthy investors, led by corporate lawyer William Shea, began work on a plan to bring another major-league franchise to New York. They could not go after an AL club because the New York Yankees refused to give up their right, under the rules of organized baseball, to veto the location of a rival AL franchise within 50 miles of Yankee Stadium. Shea and others tried, and failed, to entice an NL club to make the move. As for expansion, the owners would not listen to the idea. The ad hoc committee to return NL baseball to New York City then joined forces with Branch Rickey, who had been let go by the Pirates. Rickey had cooked up a scheme to create a third major league called the Continental League. He knew how the owners thought, and he knew that they lived in terror of Congress revoking their exemption from federal antitrust laws.

In an episode reminiscent of the great monopoly wars of the late 19th and early 20th centuries, Rickey and Shea lined up a group of well-heeled capitalists eager to buy their way into the baseball fraternity and demanded, among other things, equal access to the amateur talent pool that organized baseball controlled through the annual draft. It was not long before the major-league owners began to see the wisdom of expanding each league by two franchises—and giving one of those franchises to Joan Whitney Payson, a fabulously wealthy New York heiress who was one of the main backers of the Continental League.

In July 1960, Shea and Payson agreed, in effect, to be bought off. They dropped the Continental League plan, and Payson became the owner of a new club that would join the NL beginning with the 1962 season. She chose the name New York Mets, short for Metropolitans, which was the name of a New York team that had played in the old American Association, a major league during the 1880s. The city of New York agreed to kick in a new ballpark in Flushing, Queens—now known as Shea Stadium—that would be ready for play in 1964. In the meantime the club would play at the old Polo Grounds in Manhattan.

As for who would run the team, one day after Mrs. Payson's agreement with the NL, the Yankees fired Casey Stengel, and a few days later they fired George Weiss. The Mets hired both of them. New York was delighted. National League fans had a team to root for, and the sportswriters had Casey back. "It's a great honor," Stengel said at the 1961 press conference announcing his hiring, "for me to be joining the Knickerbockers." Whether Casey thought that he was taking over New York's basketball team, or whether he was time-tripping back through the centuries to baseball's origins in the 1840s, this was certainly not his last Stengelese pronouncement.

Expansion teams acquire players from other major-league organizations by a special draft. Each expansion draft is different, but the idea is that the existing clubs are allowed to protect their best players from the draft, exposing only middle and lower-level talent. Since it can take half a decade for a team's own amateur draft picks to mature in the minors, baseball expansion teams almost always start at the bottom. In 1962, however, it soon became clear that the NL was going to let its clubs protect all but the very dregs of their rosters. The Mets and the other expansion team, the Houston Colt .45's (now known as the Astros) were going to have to start somewhere lower than the bottom. Surveying the has-beens and the never-weres made available to them in the expansion draft, the Mets used their number one pick to select Hobert "Hobie" Landrith, a brittle backup catcher with a career batting average around .230. When asked for the reasoning behind the pick, Stengel replied, "You have to have a catcher, or you'll have a lot of passed balls."

## THE YEAR: 1962

The NL followed the AL and expanded by two teams in 1962, but all eyes were on the other end of the standings. San Francisco and Los Angeles fought a close race that came down to the final week of the season. The Giants had a slugging lineup that included Willie Mays, the NL home-run leader with 49, Orlando Cepeda, Felipe Alou, and young Willie McCovey. Jack Sanford, Juan Marichal, and Billy O'Dell led a deep pitching staff that matched up well with Los Angeles's star-studded staff of Cy Young winner Drysdale, Podres, and Koufax. The Dodgers had home-run hitters like Frank Howard, Willie Davis, and Tommy Davis, who won the NL batting title at .346 and the RBI crown with 153, but the sparkplug for the team's offense was shortstop and MVP Maury Wills, who stole a major-league record 104 bases and scored 130 runs. Los Angeles held a slim lead with a week to go, but with ERA-leader Sandy Koufax out with an injury, the team stumbled into a flat-footed tie with the Giants. Once again, the Dodgers would play a best-two-out-of-three post-season series for the NL flag. After splitting games one and two, the Dodgers led 4-2 after eight innings in game three, but still found a way to lose; the Giants scored four in the ninth to win, 6-4.

In the AL the New York Yankees won a fairly routine 96 games and another AL pennant. Mickey Mantle won another MVP award, batting .321 with 30 homers and 89 RBIs. Slugging left-fielder Harmon Killebrew led surprise contender Minnesota with a league-leading 48 home runs and 126 RBIs. Boston's Pete Runnels won the AL batting title at .326; Detroit's Hank Aguirre led in ERA at 2.21. The Yankees took a thrilling World Series from the Giants, getting a 1-0 victory in game seven when, with two out in the ninth and two men on base, Willie McCovey hit a blistering liner directly into the glove of New York second baseman Bobby Richardson.

The Mets filled their roster with such familiar big-league names as Charlie Neal, Richie Ashburn, Frank Thomas, Gene Woodling, Clem Labine, Gil Hodges, and Roger Craig. After the team played near .500 ball in spring training, some New York fans became optimistic about their team's chances. Casey Stengel, though, was not one of them. "I ain't fooled," he said, "They play different when the other side is trying too." When the regular season began, the Mets proved Casey right: When the other side was trying, they were absolutely helpless. The 1962 Mets lost the first nine games of the season. Since the Pittsburgh Pirates began the season 10–0, Stengel's club found itself 9½ games back before they had learned each others' names. Things got worse. The club had a few respectable players: Frank Thomas hit 34 home runs and drove in 94 runs, and Richie Ashburn hit .306. Most of the Mets, however, had at least one thing seriously wrong with them. Bumbling first baseman Marv Throneberry had hands of stone. Catcher Chris Cannizzaro could not hit. Hodges and Labine were too banged up to play. And none of the Mets could pitch. The team ERA leader, Al Jackson, went 8–20 with an ERA of 4.40; Roger Craig went 10–24 with an ERA of 4.51. The Mets as a whole went 40–120 to finish an unbelievable 60½ games behind.

*Mets manager Casey Stengel seems to be saying "What Can I Do?" as he talks to reporters before a 1962 game. The expansion Mets went on to lose that day—the team's fifteenth straight loss—on its way to a wretched 40–120 season.*

The 1962 Mets were, as Casey Stengel called them, "amazin'." They were so bad, in fact, that they became fashionable. The "Amazin' Mets" became a popular catchphrase. "Come out and see my amazin' Mets," Stengel would say. "I been in this game a hundred years but I see new ways to lose I never knew existed before." Whether it was Stengel's personal charisma or a phenomenon of the iconoclastic 1960s, New York fell in love with the team that could not hit, run, field, or throw. After the team's first bench-clearing brawl, one sportswriter commented that they could not fight, either.

The Mets seemed to be the perfect alternative to the pompous, corporate Yankees. New York fans came out to the Polo Grounds, chanted "Let's Go Mets!" and traded their favorite Mets anecdotes. There was the time that the team was celebrating Throneberry's birthday, and Casey Stengel cut everyone a piece of cake except for Throneberry himself. "We wuz afraid," Stengel explained, "that he'd drop it." There was the story of how center fielder Ashburn was having trouble communicating with Spanish-speaking second baseman Elio Chacon on fly balls to short right-center. Teammate Joe Christopher suggested that Ashburn call for the ball in Spanish by saying "Yo la tengo" instead of "I've got it." The first time Ashburn tried it in a game, however, 6 foot 3 inch, 225-pound right fielder Frank Thomas ran him over like a Mack truck. Told that he had been voted "Most Valuable Met" by the team's fans, Ashburn paused and said: "Just how do they mean that?"

In a year in which they lost more games than any major-league club since the 1899 Cleveland Spiders, the New York Mets drew 922,530 fans, more than seven other big-league teams and only half a million fewer than the mighty Yankees. This turned out to be just the beginning. The New York Mets continued to lose in 1963, 1964, and 1965, but saw their attendance double. Starting in 1964, the awful Mets began a string of twelve consecutive years in which they outdrew the Yankees. As the Mets achieved respectability and then won the 1969 world championship, the Yankees dropped into the second division to stay and were sold again, this time to Cleveland ship-

*On April 10, 1965, Jim Beauchamp is congratulated by his Houston teammates after hitting the team's first home run in the Astrodome. The Astrodome—the major league's first domed stadium—provided a look into the future of baseball.*

builder George Steinbrenner. With Houston also drawing well, expansion had proven to be an unqualified success. Thanks in large part to three baseball men who had been let go by the owners because they were too old, organized baseball was being dragged, kicking and screaming, into the future.

# Source Notes

CHAPTER ONE
1. John Tullius, *I'd Rather Be a Yankee* (New York: Macmillan, 1986), p. 183.
2. Ibid., pp. 223–34.
3. Bill James, *The Bill James Historical Baseball Abstract* (New York: Villard, 1988), p.206.
4. Tullius, p. 238.
5. Ibid., p. 239.

CHAPTER TWO
1. Kevin Kerrane, *Dollar Sign on the Muscle* (New York: Beaufort, 1984), pp. 16–17.
2. Mickey Mantle and Lewis Early, *Mickey Mantle* (Chicago: Sagamore, 1996), p. 21.
3. Tullius, p. 226.

CHAPTER THREE
1. Peter Golenbock, *Bums* (New York: Putnam, 1984), p. 283.

CHAPTER FOUR
1. Roger Kahn, *The Boys of Summer* (New York: Harper and Row, 1971), p. xix.
2. Golenbock, p. 57.

CHAPTER FIVE
1. John Tullius, p. 228.

CHAPTER SIX
1. Charles Einstein, *Willie's Time* (New York: Penguin, 1992), p. 34.

CHAPTER EIGHT
1. Tullius, p. 261.

# Bibliography

Allen, Lee. *The American League Story*. New York: Hill and Wang, 1962.
_____. *The National League Story*. New York: Hill and Wang, 1961.
Allen, Maury. *Roger Maris*. New York: Fine, 1986.
Anderson, Dave. *Pennant Races*. New York: Doubleday, 1994.
Creamer, Robert. *Stengel*. New York: Simon and Schuster, 1984.
Durocher, Leo. *Nice Guys Finish Last*. New York: Simon and Schuster, 1975.
Goldstein, Richard. *Superstars and Screwballs*. New York, Dutton, 1991.
Golenbock, Peter. *Bums*. New York: Putnam, 1984.
James, Bill. *The Bill James Historical Baseball Abstract*. New York: Villard, 1988.
Kahn, Roger. *The Boys of Summer*. New York: Harper and Row, 1971.
Koppett, Leonard. *The Man in the Dugout*. New York: Crown, 1993.
Lieb, Fred. *The Story of the World Series*. New York: Putnam, 1965.
Moffi, Larry, and Jonathan Kronstadt. *Crossing the Line*. Iowa City: University of Iowa Press, 1994.
Reichler, Joseph, ed. *The Baseball Encyclopedia*. New York: Macmillan, 1988.
Robinson, Frank and Berry Stainback. *Extra Innings*. New York: McGraw-Hill, 1988.
Robinson, Jackie. *I Never Had It Made*. New York: Putnam, 1972.
Thorn, John, and Pete Palmer, eds. *Total Baseball*. 3d ed. New York: HarperCollins, 1993.
Thomson, Bobby, with Lee Heiman and Bill Gutman. *The Giants Win the Pennant! The Giants Win the Pennant!* New York: Kensington, 1991.
Tullius, John. *I'd Rather Be a Yankee*. New York: Macmillan, 1986.
Tygiel, Jules. *Baseball's Great Experiment*. New York: Oxford University Press, 1983.

# Index

139

Marshall, Willard, 52
Martin, Billy, 13, 38–42, 63, 67, 85, 90, 93
Mathews, Eddie, 40, 68, 98, 114, 116
Mays, Willie, 39, 42, 53–54, 56, 59, 71, 74, *82–83*, 84, 87, *96*, 98, 100–102, 115, 131
Mazeroski, Bill, 120, *121*
McCarthy, Joe, 5, 16, 23
McCormick, Mike, 120
McCovey, Willie, 131–32
McDougald, Gil, 86, 90, 97
McGraw, Blanche, 48
McGraw, John, 8, 13, 48–49
Medwick, Joe, 63
Meyers, John "Chief," 49
Miller, Stu, 114, 116
Milwaukee Braves, 40, 67, 76, 91, 98, 114–16
Milwaukee Brewers, 9
Minnesota Twins, 125
Minoso, Orestes "Minnie," 36, 67, 94, 98, 100, 107
Mize, Johnny, 11, 21, 52, 90, 92
Moffi, Larry, 101
Monroe, Marilyn, 34
Moon, Wally, 116
Moore, JoJo, 49
Moses, Robert, 115
Moss, Don, 27
Mossi, Don, 84
Mueller, Don, 57–58
Mullin, Willard, 62, 76
Murderers' Row, 23
Musial, Stan, 10, 21, 37–38, 64, 91
*My Favorite Summer*, 45

Narleski, Ray, 27, 84
Neal, Charlie, 116, 132
Negro Leagues, 70-71, 74, 99–101, 105
New York Giants, 7, 37, 39, 48-61, 65, 84, 100, 102, 111, 114
New York Mets, 8, 117, 129–34
Newcombe, Don, 27, 37, 53, 55–58, 66, 75, 84, 87, 91, 94

Newfield, Jack, 115
Newhouser, Hal, 27, 84
Newsom, Bobo, 78
Niarhos, Gus, 15
Nichols, Chet, 37
Niemann, Bob, 24

Oakland Oaks, 9, 13, 40
O'Dell, Billy, 131
O'Malley, Peter, 115
O'Malley, Walter, 91, 111–12, 114–15, 117, 119
O'Toole, Jim, 126
Ott, Mel, 49
Owen, Mickey, 63

Pafko, Andy, 55, 57, 59, 68, 72, 86, 90
Page, Joe, 11-12, 14, 16
Paige, Satchel, 94, 97, 110
Parnell, Mel, 15–16
Payson, Joan Whitney, 130
Perini, Lou, 67, 111
Pesky, Johnny, 11, 22
Philadelphia Athletics, 111
Philadelphia Phillies, 8, 10, 21–22, 39
Pierce, Billy, 87
Pinson, Vada, 126
Pittsburgh Pirates, 11, 118–20, 132
platooning, 13
Podres, Johnny, 27, 76, 98, 131
Pollet, Howie, 11
Polo Grounds, 48, 55, 58–59, *113*
Post, Wally, 126

Raschi, Vic, 11, 13–14, 17, 36, 39, 89, 91-92
Reese, Harold "Pee Wee," 27, 53, 55, 57, 58, 62, 64, *68*, 69–70, 82, 86, 89–90, 92
Reiser, Pete, 63, 72
Reserve clause, 45–46
Reynolds, Allie, 11, 12, 14, 16, 36, 39, 86, 89, 92
Rhodes, James "Dusty", 84
Richardson, Bobby, 23, 97, 119, 132

# About the Author

Thomas Gilbert has published many books and articles on baseball history, as well as a biography of Roberto Clemente. For Franklin Watts, he has written *Baseball and the Color Line* and the previous titles in this series—*Elysian Fields, Superstars and Monopoly Wars, Dead Ball, The Soaring Twenties, The Good Old Days,* and *Baseball at War.* Mr. Gilbert lives in Brooklyn, New York.